The Heritage Sampler

The HERITAGE SAMPLER

A Book of Colonial Arts & Crafts

by CHERYL G. HOOPLE

pictures and diagrams by Richard Cuffari

THE DIAL PRESS · NEW YORK

Text copyright © 1975 by Cheryl Hoople • Pictures copyright ©
1975 by Richard Cuffari • All rights reserved • No part of this book
may be reproduced in any form or by any means without the prior
written permission of the publisher, excepting brief quotes used in
connection with reviews written specifically for inclusion in a
magazine or newspaper • Printed in the United States of America
First Printing • Designed by Jane Byers Bierhorst

Library of Congress Cataloging in Publication Data

Hoople, Cheryl G
The heritage sampler.

Bibliography: p.
1. Handicraft—United States—History—Juvenile literature.
2. United States—History—Colonial period, ca. 1600–1775—
Juvenile literature. 3. Cookery—Juvenile literature. [1. Handicraft.
2. United States—Social life and customs—Colonial period, ca.
1600–1775. 3. Cookery] I. Cuffari, Richard, 1925–   II. Title.
TT23.H66   745.5'0973   75–9203
ISBN 0–8037–5414–0 • ISBN 0–8037–5430–2 lib. bdg.

*For my children Carrie and Joey, and
their children's children*

Contents

Introduction

The first European immigrants to the wild, wind-swept coast of America came to Plymouth in Massachusetts, to New Netherland, which is now New York, to the Middle Colonies such as Pennsylvania and Delaware, and to Virginia and the Carolinas. They came for a dozen different reasons—religious freedom, wealth and land, a new life and greener pastures—but they all faced the same challenge of survival in an unknown land thousands of miles from their former homes.

Surviving in a new land was difficult, but with the help of friendly Indians, the newcomers learned how to gather shellfish and grow corn, where to hunt, and where to gather wild berries and healthful herbs. They made new homes. Some dug caves in the hills or copied the Indians and built dome-shaped wigwams; others stretched sailcloth over poles or chopped trees and raised log stockades. Later they erected neat towns with frame houses and brick and stone mills and stores, towns where bakers and bankers, parsons and printers lived. By 1733 there were thirteen colonies.

Life in America called for new ways of thinking and of making things—not only houses, but roads and muskets, locks, clocks, and Conestoga wagons. Through trial and error, hard work and sweat, the early colonists developed by necessity a talent for fixing things and making do. A pioneer in the New World had to be a farmer, carpenter, merchant, and scout, to know something about crops, weather, and livestock. He or she had to know how to preserve food, dip candles, weave cloth, and cure ills. Even children worked hard sewing quilts, shearing sheep, herding, and hoeing.

In *The Heritage Sampler: A Book of Colonial Arts and Crafts,* you can find out how the early colonists lived in the years when all one needed grew in the woods and fields. Try your hand at weaving, pouring candles, making bread, sewing rag dolls, embroidering friendship pillows, drawing silhouettes, and braiding cornhusk mats. Pioneers used these crafts and many more to make a home for themselves in the wilderness, but today you can simply have fun doing them your way.

The Heritage Sampler

1

Beside the Fire

Settlers in the New World rose before dawn, poked the hot coals buried in yesterday's ashes, and put the kettle on. Soon the smell of bacon, tea, and mush reached the sleepyheads and one by one, they crawled down the ladder from the loft. Everyone had a job to do. Some dressed the little ones and set the table; others filled the woodbox and fed the animals. Then the head of the house gathered everyone together and said the blessing.

A colonial kitchen was the heart of the household and in many early homes, the only room. Here people slept, ate, worked, and played. Women spent most of the day there cooking on a fire, turning out mouth-watering meals with only a few cooking utensils, spoons, and bowls. A simple bread pudding was a frontier favorite; here is a recipe from an old cookbook. You may find it hard to understand!

Sieve one pound of soft bread soaked in one quart of milk; crack seven eggs, ¾ pound sugar, ¼ pound butter, spices and salt; plump one pound stoned raisins in one gill of rose-water; ½ pint of cream. Mix all together and bake one hour in a middling oven.

The fireplace usually covered an entire wall and had a swinging iron crane built inside the chimney on which cooking pots were hung. Some heavy kettles weighed forty pounds. A stack of dry kindling was kept near the hearth to start a fire quickly; chunks of slow-burning hard wood were then added. A full hour would pass before the fire died down leaving a bed of coals to cook on.

To broil meat, the cook held a slice over the hot coals on the end of a long-handled fork or put a large cut on a spit and slowly turned it for three or four hours. Potatoes, corn, nuts, and onions were buried in hot ashes and roasted.

One day a week a family baked a seven-day supply of bread. First they filled the oven built into the side of the chimney with glowing embers from the fire. To test the oven's temperature, they put one hand inside and counted "one, two, three . . ." If they could hold the hand inside to the full count of ten, they knew the oven was hot enough to bake but not so hot that it would burn their juicy berry pies and loaves of bread. Children helped push the plump loaves into the oven with wide wooden shovels called peels.

Early colonists ate in front of the fire at a long trestle table lined with hard, backless benches. Because they usually ate soups and spoon-meat—

meat made into stew and hash—they used only a spoon and often held their food in their hands. A wooden noggin or mug held the stew and vegetables, and a pewter tankard held the drink. No forks or china to wash, but lots of napkins!

Fireside Recipes

CORNBREAD

MATERIALS

8-inch square pan or a loaf pan   *sifter*
measuring cups and spoons   *large and small mixing bowls*
small saucepan   *large spoon*

INGREDIENTS

shortening   *3 teaspoons baking powder*
3 tablespoons butter   *1 ¼ cups cornmeal*
¾ cup all-purpose flour   *1 egg*
¼ cup sugar   *¾ cup milk*
¾ teaspoon salt

1 • Pre-heat oven to 425°F. Grease the pan with a little shortening or butter and put it in the oven to heat until the shortening sizzles. Melt 3 tablespoons butter in a small saucepan over a low heat.

2 • While the baking pan heats and the butter melts, sift together ¾ cup all-purpose flour, ¼ cup sugar, ¾ teaspoon salt, and 3 teaspoons baking powder into a large mixing bowl. Add 1 ¼ cups cornmeal.

3 • Beat one egg in a small bowl and then mix in 3 tablespoons melted butter and ¾ cup milk.

4 • Pour the egg, butter, and milk into the flour and sugar. Stir with a few strokes. The batter will be slightly lumpy. Put the batter in the hot pan and bake for about 25 minutes.

5 • The cornbread is ready to eat when a toothpick pushed into the center of the bread comes out clean. Cut and eat warm with butter.

JOHNNYCAKES

MATERIALS

saucepan   *waxed paper*
large spoon   *greased baking sheet*

INGREDIENTS

5 teaspoons butter   *3 cups water*
1½ cups yellow cornmeal   *¾ teaspoon salt*

1 • Pre-heat oven to 400°F.

2 • Melt the butter in a saucepan.

3 • Add all the other ingredients and cook, stirring constantly, until the mixture thickens and the cornmeal batter has absorbed all the water.

4 • Remove the pan from the stove. Place a piece of waxed paper over the saucepan and let the batter cool about 20 to 30 minutes, until you can hold the cornmeal in your hands.

5 • Shape the mixture into patties about ½ inch thick and put them on a greased baking sheet. Bake for about 25 minutes.

6 • Eat with dabs of butter and pancake syrup.

HOT SPICED CIDER

MATERIALS

large pot with a lid
measuring cups and spoons
string and a square of

cheesecloth, or strainer
long-handled spoon
serving cups

INGREDIENTS

½ *gallon sweet apple cider*
½ *cup brown sugar*
1 *teaspoon each whole cloves*

and allspice
1 *cinnamon stick*

1 • Pour the ½ gallon of sweet cider into a large pot. Add ½ cup brown sugar and stir with a long-handled spoon.

2 • Tie up the whole cloves, allspice, and cinnamon stick in a small square of cheesecloth and drop into the cider. Cover the pot and slowly bring the mixture to a boil. Lower the heat and gently simmer the mixture for about 20 minutes.

3 • Remove the spice bag and serve in warmed cups. If you do not use cheesecloth, drop the spices into the cider, simmer, and strain the liquid before serving. This will fill about 8 cups.

APPLE FRITTERS

MATERIALS

knife	*sifter*
measuring cups and spoons	*paper towels*
small saucepan	*frying pan*
mixing bowl	*wide spatula*
fork	

INGREDIENTS

6 apples	*dash of salt*
1 tablespoon butter	*1 tablespoon sugar*
2 eggs	*shortening*
½ cup milk	*powdered sugar, syrup, or jam*
1 cup all-purpose flour	

1 • Peel the apples. Remove the core and seeds from the center and slice them into ¼-inch thick apple rings.

2 • Melt 1 tablespoon butter in a saucepan and set aside to let it cool. Lightly beat 2 eggs in a bowl; add ½ cup milk and beat again.

3 • Sift 1 cup flour, add a dash of salt and 1 tablespoon sugar, and combine with the liquid. Mix until smooth with as few strokes as possible. Add the melted butter and blend.

4 • The batter should drop in splats from a spoon. If it is too thick, add a little more milk; if the batter is too thin, add more flour.

5 • Rinse the peeled apple rings in water and dry them on paper towels. Dip the rings into the batter and fry them on both sides in a hot, greased frying pan until crisp and golden brown. Use just enough shortening to keep the fritters from sticking. Drain the fritters on paper towels to get rid of excess grease.

6 • Sprinkle with powdered sugar or spread with jam or syrup and eat warm.

IRISH SODA BREAD

MATERIALS

sifter
large mixing bowl
measuring cups and spoons
knife and fork

mixing spoon
greased 9 x 5-inch loaf pan
*   or an 8-inch cake or pie pan*

INGREDIENTS

2 cups all-purpose flour
¾ teaspoon baking soda
½ teaspoon salt
1 tablespoon sugar

6 tablespoons shortening
¾ cup raisins
⅔ cup buttermilk

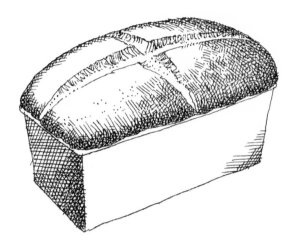

1 • Pre-heat oven to 375°F. Sift together into a large bowl 2 cups all-purpose flour, ¾ teaspoon baking soda, ½ teaspoon salt, and 1 tablespoon sugar.

2 • Cut 6 tablespoons shortening into the flour mixture with a knife and fork. Cut the flour and shortening as you would a piece of meat until the pieces are the size of small peas.

3 • Stir in ¾ cup raisins and gradually add ⅔ cup buttermilk. Stir again until blended.

4 • Sprinkle about ½ cup of flour on a board or kitchen counter. Dust your hands with flour and turn out the dough onto the floured surface.

5 • To knead, fold the dough toward you with your fingers and then push it away with the heel of your hand. Keep your hands and dough lightly coated with flour as you knead. Knead the dough for about 5 minutes.

6 • Gently shape the dough to fit the greased pan. Cut a bold cross, about ½-inch deep in the middle, across the top of the loaf with a sharp knife. Make the cross touch the sides of the pan, so the bread will not crack in baking.

7 · Gently brush buttermilk over the top of the dough with your fingers. Bake for about 50 minutes. The bread is done when a toothpick pushed into the center of the bread comes out clean.

This simple recipe makes delicious skillet bread on an open fire or on your kitchen stove. Lightly rub a heavy skillet with shortening. Put the bread dough in the greased pan, cut a cross, and cover with a lid. Cook over a low heat for about 30 minutes. Be careful not to burn the bottom of the bread.

2

"Come Butter Come"

The cow held a place of honor in early America. In lean years when the crops failed and people had no money, they bartered her butter and cheese for the goods they needed—barrels and meal, shoes and thread. Not everyone owned a cow. Butter was a luxury. On those rare mornings when there was butter for the griddle cakes, even the sleepiest child tumbled from his pallet in the loft and scrambled down the ladder to breakfast.

Children usually cared for the stock and it was their job to herd "Old Betsy" home each night. They brought the milk pails to the house after milking and poured the warm milk into wooden tubs or trays. As the milk soured, they skimmed off the cream from the top and emptied it into the butter churn. Most churns looked like tall wooden buckets, stiff as soldiers and narrow at the top.

When enough cream collected in the churn, the girls or boys put in a long round stick called a dasher, and they were ready to make butter. Up and down, up and down they pushed the dasher. First the cream bubbled and foamed, and then turned into a mass of floating lumps or curds.

Churning butter was hard work. To pass the time, the churner chanted rhymes to the rhythm of the dasher. A favorite chant went:

> Come butter come
> Come butter come
> Peter standing at the gate
> Waiting for a butter cake
> Come butter come.

Twenty, thirty, or forty minutes passed. When the butter finally came, the churner cleaned the butter from the dasher, rinsed the butter with cold water, and added salt for flavor. The liquid that remained was buttermilk, delicious to drink. Working with two wooden paddles, the churner then shaped the newly made butter into squares, wrapped them, and packed them into tubs called firkins.

Some settlers measured their butter in half-pound- or pound-sized butter molds. These round wooden molds pressed a design into the butter. Sometimes butter makers chose a shock of wheat, a thistle, an eagle, or a star as a personal design, and it became their trademark. Anyone who bought their butter knew who had made it.

HOMEMADE BUTTER

MATERIALS

clean, quart-sized glass jar with   *4–5 ice cubes*
   a screw-top lid   *butter dish*
mixing bowl

INGREDIENTS

2 cups whipping cream   ¼ *teaspoon salt*

1 • Remove the cream from the refrigerator and place it and the glass jar in a warm place near the stove or in the sun for about two hours.

2 • Put the warm cream in the jar and screw the lid on tight. Hold the jar by the ends between your hands and shake up and down for 10 to 20 minutes. Try chanting "Come Butter Come" or make up a rhyme of your own to pass the time. Take turns with a friend.

3 • When the butter gathers or "comes," it will stick together and form a solid mass. (If the butter balls will not stick together, add several teaspoons of hot water.) Pour off the buttermilk and put the butter into a mixing bowl.

4 • Wash your hands with soap and water. Put the ice cubes in the bowl and let the ice melt a little. Work the water into the butter with your fingers until the butter is cold. Pour off the ice cubes and water.

5 • Sprinkle ¼ teaspoon salt over the cold butter and mix thoroughly with your fingers until the salt disappears.

6 • Shape the butter into a square, circle, or triangle, a cat, bear, or dog. Think up your own design. Put it on a dish and place in the refrigerator to harden.

3

Quilting Bee

On December nights when snow sifted through the cabin cracks, frontier children burrowed deep inside the quilts piled high on their beds. Thank goodness mothers, aunts, and grannies spent so many hours sewing quilts to keep them cozy warm. Women often kept a basket beside their chair filled with cloth scraps. In the evening they sat near the fire and cut them into squares, triangles, and circles, and sorted and arranged them into beautiful designs.

It took many scraps to make one quilted "kiver," but all good quilters knew the history and origin of every scrap in their quilts: red squares from Mary's old Sunday dress, brown circles from Grandma's everyday skirt, and blue linsey-woolsey blocks from brother Ben's coat. Girls helped, too, and learned their first stitches sewing quilts.

When the top had been pieced together, a layer of goose down or wool was sandwiched between a cloth backing and the colorful top, and all three layers were stretched over a four-sided wooden frame. Then the neighbors were invited to a quilting bee. The quilters arrived early with basket lunches and stayed all day. Up and down, in and out, the needles flew. Quilting demanded nimble fingers and good eyesight. The simplest quilting held the layers of cloth together with closely spaced parallel or crisscross rows of tiny running stitches, but sometimes the quilting was done in intricate shapes and patterns—baskets, flowers, and birds.

Every pattern had a name: "Delectable Mountains," "Wild Goose Chase," "Shoo Fly," "Buzzard's Roost," and "The Rocky Road to Kansas," as well as "Dixie Rose," "Yankee Pride," "The Bird of Paradise," and dozens more. Bright colors bloomed like a spring bouquet on the colonists' beds. Even when stained, yellowed, and aged, handmade quilts were family treasures.

In pioneer America, women made quilts from cradle to grave. Before she married, a young girl had at least a dozen quilts for everyday use and a special one for her wedding day. Some people said if a young girl slept under a new quilt, she dreamed of the boy she would marry.

PATCHWORK PILLOW

MATERIALS

scissors
ruler

needle
strong thread

chalk
enough scrap material to make nine
  5 x 5-inch cloth squares
straight pins

1 yard of fabric
½ yard cotton or dacron batting,
  or a thin blanket or piece of wool
foam pillow stuffing or old rags

1 • Use scraps of leftover cloth. A variety of plain colored, plaid, or print fabrics will make your pillow colorful and bright. Cut the scrap material into nine squares, each 5 inches long and 5 inches wide. Arrange the squares in different color combinations to find the patchwork pattern you like best.

The design for this pillow is called a nine-patch because the patches are laid out three squares down and three squares across to make a large block.

2 • Sew the nine squares, arranged in rows of three, together with a running stitch (see illustration below). First pin two squares together with the wrong side out. Sew along one edge with small, even stitches. Open the squares out flat.

Quilting Stitches

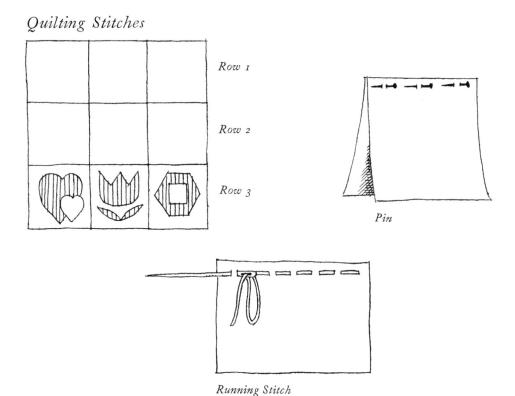

Row 1

Row 2

Row 3

Pin

Running Stitch

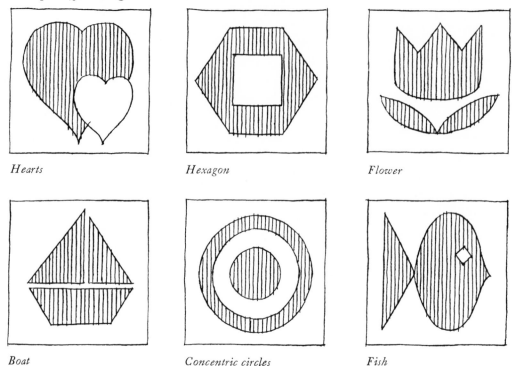

Hearts   *Hexagon*   *Flower*

Boat   *Concentric circles*   *Fish*

Then pin and sew the third square in the first row to one of the two squares just completed. Repeat for the second and third row. Make sure all the right sides are facing the same way. Then sew the second row of three patches to the first row and finally, the third row to the first two. Press the seams open. Now you have a patchwork block of nine squares that will be your quilted pillow top.

3 • Cut a piece the same size as the top of the pillow from the yard of cloth. Also cut a piece of cotton or dacron batting or a thin blanket or a piece of wool the same size as your pillow top. This batting will be the filler between the cloth layers. Put it between your piece of cloth and the patchwork squares. Pin the three layers together so they won't slip.

4 • To quilt the pillow top, choose one or more of the sample patterns or design

a pattern of your own. Draw lightly with chalk one pattern inside each patch-work square. Or choose an overall pattern that covers all nine squares, such as several concentric circles (see illustration on p. 20). You can use a compass to draw the circles. Outline each pattern with small, even running stitches (see illustration on p. 19). Push the needle up and down through all three layers of cloth.

5 • Cut another piece of cloth the same size as the quilted top. Put the two pieces together with the wrong sides out. Sew a ½-inch seam around three sides and four corners with the running stitch. Leave about an 8-inch opening on the bottom edge. Turn right sides out.

6 • Fill the pillow with clean old rags or foam pillow stuffing. Close the opening with tiny, almost invisible stitches.

4

Harvest Home

Gathering a day's supply of food in the New World was never easy. Food spoiled rapidly without refrigeration, so many colonists built a trough in a nearby stream where they put leftover meat, milk, and fresh vegetables. The shallow water ran over the buried crocks and pans and kept the food cold even on the hottest summer day. Buckets of fresh drinking water were drawn from the same stream. No one had hot and cold running water in the house.

Colonists feared the Starving Times, the last weeks of winter. In the fall they filled the root cellar with pickled vegetables, smoked meat, and dried fruit, but by early spring the food cache dwindled to a few wilted greens and rotten shanks of meat. Faced with hunger, they ate wild herbs, milkweed, and nettles until the first plants bore fruit.

Everyone prepared for winter all the rest of the year. Women pickled green walnuts, nasturtium buds, parsley, and mushrooms; grapes were buried in wood ashes and lemons were dipped in wax to seal the rind and juice. Children worked too. They caught fish and game to salt and "powder" with spices in tubs and helped their elders smoke ham and bacon over slow corncob and hickory-chip fires.

Just before the first frost young and old pulled up turnips, carrots, and cabbage and carted them to the root cellar, built partially below ground and walled with earth and stones. Later they added apples, freshly dug potatoes, and crocks of heavily spiced fruit and wild berries. The children also gathered fallen nuts.

European settlers learned the Indian way to sun-dry food. The shriveled meat, vegetables, and fruit plumped up and tasted almost fresh after they were soaked in water and cooked. Apples, peaches, and pears were peeled and sliced and laid on a clean sheet in the sun to dry. At night they were brought inside. After two or three weeks of drying, the fruit was stored in covered baskets, crocks, and gourds. Even peppers, beans, and peas dried well in the sun or on a string by the fire.

DRIED FRUIT AND VEGETABLES

MATERIALS

clean, old sheet

sharp knife

needle

several coat hangers

broomstick or long wooden pole

piece of cheesecloth

heavy-duty thread   *containers with lids*
scissors   *saucepan*

INGREDIENTS

vegetables—peas, corn, green beans, or   *fruit—apples, blueberries, blackberries,*
  peppers   *peaches, or apricots*

Vegetables take six to twelve hours to dry, depending on the size of the pieces and the amount of humidity in the air. Fruits take eight hours or longer to dry. Dried fruit feels dry and leathery on the outside but slightly moist inside. Vegetables should be brittle.

Peas

Shell and lay ripe peas on a clean sheet in the sun to dry. Bring them inside at night. The hulls will crack. When the peas are dry, tap them with the side of a knife to remove the loose hulls. Store the peas in a closed container. To use, soak the peas in water to soften, and then cook them.

Corn

Husk and clean ears of corn. Cut the corn off the cob with a sharp knife and dry the kernels in the sun on a clean sheet. Store the dried corn in a closed container.

Green Beans

String green beans on a length of strong thread and hang in a warm, shaded place. Hang until the beans dry and store them in a closed container until used.

Peppers

Wash and string hot red peppers with a needle on a length of strong thread.

Try long red cayenne or chili peppers. Make several pepper strings, tie them on a coat hanger, and put it in an airy closet to dry. A dried pepper skin feels dry and wrinkled. Strings of dried peppers hung in every colonial kitchen as food and decoration. Add a bright yarn or ribbon bow and give a pepper string as a gift or hang it in your home.

Fruit and Berries

Peel and slice apples into slivers or core peeled apples and cut into ½-inch thick rings. String the rings on a broom handle or on a pole and hang in the sun. String apple slivers on a length of strong thread and hang, or lay apple slivers and rings on a clean sheet in the sun to dry. You can peel, slice, and dry peaches and apricots in this way; whole blueberries and blackberries can be spread on a sheet to dry. Apples and other fruit will turn brown and rubbery. Cover the fruit you dry outside with cheesecloth or lightweight cloth to protect it from dirt and insects. Store dried fruit in closed containers. You also can heat dried slices in a 225°F. oven for about 5 minutes to kill any germs.

To cook dried fruit and vegetables, you must replace the water taken out during the drying process. Pour about 1½ cups of boiling water over 1 cup of dried food. Let the food absorb the water until it will hold no more. Dried vegetables usually soak up enough water in about two hours, but fruits usually take longer, from two to four hours or more. You can bake the fruit in pies and other desserts.

Or try this dried fruit treat:

Grind ½ pound each raisins, dates, dried apricots, dried apples, and dried peaches or pears in a meat grinder or chop very fine. Grind or chop 2 cups nuts. Mix the fruit and nuts together with your hands in just enough honey to hold the fruit together. Don't make it too sticky. Roll the fruit mix into teaspoon-sized balls and roll in powdered sugar or graham cracker crumbs. Put the dried fruit balls on waxed paper to dry. Store in a sealed container. Makes about 7 dozen balls that will keep for a month.

ROASTED NUTS

MATERIALS

1 bag of nuts (walnuts, hickory nuts,
*   filberts, pecans, peanuts,*
*   or chestnuts)*
nutcracker
mixing bowl
measuring cups and spoons

melted butter or oil (peanut,
*   sesame, or safflower)*
mixing spoon
cookie sheet or heavy-bottomed skillet
salt
hot pads

1 • Pre-heat oven to 350°F. Shell the nuts and put them in a bowl. Sprinkle over them 1 teaspoon of melted butter or oil for every cup of nuts in the bowl. Stir the nuts to coat them with the oil.

2 • Spread the nuts on a cookie sheet and sprinkle them lightly with salt. Roast the nuts for about 10 minutes. Carefully watch them so they won't turn dark. They should lightly brown and roast. Cool and eat!

3 • You can also roast nuts on an open fire outdoors. Follow step 1; then put the nuts and several tablespoons of butter and oil in a heavy-bottomed skillet.

Roast the nuts over the fire's coals for about 10 minutes. Carefully stir the nuts so they won't burn. Add more butter or oil to the skillet to keep the nuts from sticking, if necessary.

Hard-rinded gourds sown from seeds in mounds of fertile dirt grew in every frontier garden. They grew in different shapes, colors, and sizes. While Indians danced to gourd drums, babies shook gourd rattles, and housewives darned stockings with hollow gourd "eggs" and served soup in gourd bowls. Many a mountain man tapped his boot to the music of a gourd fiddle.

GOURD DOODADS

MATERIALS

seed packet of mixed ornamental gourds or mature gourds
hammer
small nail
newspaper
soft cloth
small hand saw

wooden plug, cork, or dried corncob (for gourd bottles)
bottle of liquid self-polishing wax
toothbrush or old paint brush (to apply wax)
sandpaper

1 • Grow your own gourds or buy them in a store. Make a small hole with a hammer and nail in the bottom of the gourds. Put one hole in the soft spot on the stem or blossom end. If you are planning to make a bottle, put a hole only in the stem end.

2 • Lay the gourds on sheets of newspaper in an airy, shaded spot. Every morn-

ing use a soft cloth to wipe off the moisture that has condensed on the gourds and turn them over. Gourds take about two-and-a-half weeks to four months to dry, depending on size and shell thickness. They are cured when the seeds rattle inside when you shake the shell.

3 · When the gourds are dry, use a small hand saw to cut round or oval ones in half to make bowls and containers. Sand the rough edges. Leave the seeds inside small dried gourds to make baby rattles. Long gourds with bulbous ends make good dippers, if you cut the rounded end in half; or cut off the pointed end and insert a wooden plug, cork, or dried corncob to make a bottle. Colorful, warted, and irregular-shaped gourds heaped in baskets or tied together make beautiful ornaments and wall decorations.

4 · Brush a coat of liquid self-polishing wax on dried gourds. Buff and shine them with a cloth. Apply several coats, but be sure you carve the gourds *before* you wax the shells.

5

Husking Bee

The first Europeans in New World communities learned about corn from peaceful Indians who brought them popped corn as a token of goodwill. No one in Europe ate or planted corn, so the Indians taught the early colonists to put five corn kernels together in a mound of earth—one for the worms, two for the crows, one to die, and one to grow. Observant settlers learned many uses for corn from their Indian friends.

Indian women placed dry corn kernels on hot stones or tossed them into hot ashes and let them pop out. They ground corn to make corn cakes and mush. Soon pioneer families ate bowls of hot porridge made from cornmeal and milk. Sometimes they crushed and boiled kernels to make "samp" or parched dried corn for a winter evening treat. Pounded parched corn could be carried in a knapsack on hunting trips. Some people said a person could live on three spoonfuls a day.

New World pioneers took pride in their gardens and crops. Corn came first, and the rows of turned earth had to be just so, perfectly straight and even. As soon as the young corn plants came up, pesky squirrels and crows raided the rows. Every morning the children had to chase them away with stones and clubs. By late August the colonists had corn to trade and roast. Homemakers stuffed new mattress ticks and braided baskets and floor mats with cornhusks. Farmers left the choicest ears on the stalk to dry. Later they tied them together in threes and fours and hung them in the rafters to wait for winter popping. Colonists also paid taxes with corn. They even voted with corn in their town meetings. A corn kernel cast a "yea" vote, a bean cast a "nay" vote.

With October weather came the full moon called the hunter's moon, and plans for a husking bee were made. After the harvesters heaped the ears into a long pile, the neighbors gathered. Team captains paced the corn pile to find the line that marked the middle. Then they rallied their sides and raced through the stack tossing husked ears to the center.

Shouts and laughter echoed into the night. A lucky husker who found a red ear of corn got to kiss the girl of his choice. Sometimes a zealous fellow smuggled a red ear into the husking. At the right moment, he pulled it from under his coat and claimed his kiss. When the last ear was shucked, everyone ate the feast laid on nearby tables. In later years a fiddler turned the tunes and called the steps as everyone danced till early morn.

POPPED CORN

MATERIALS

heavy skillet or electric skillet   large mixing bowl
measuring cups and spoons

INGREDIENTS

4 teaspoons peanut or corn oil   ¼ teaspoon salt
½ cup popping corn   2 tablespoons or more melted butter

1 • Pre-heat the heavy skillet over high heat or heat the electric skillet to 400°F. Add 2 teaspoons peanut or corn oil to the hot skillet for each ¼ cup corn. For light, fluffy popcorn never overload the skillet, so only pop ¼ cup corn at a time.

2 • Keep the skillet covered and moving constantly so the corn will not burn. If the kernels have the proper moisture content, you can hear them start to pop in about one minute. One minute more and you have a pan of popped corn. Throw away burned kernels and empty the popped corn into a large bowl. One-half cup of corn makes about 4 cups of popped corn.

3 • Gently sprinkle ¼ teaspoon salt over 4 cups of popped corn, add 2 tablespoons or more melted butter, toss lightly, and you have a campfire favorite.

Try this variation on the old-time recipe:

MATERIALS

double boiler   large bowl
long-handled wooden spoon   spoon
measuring cups and spoons   cookie sheet

INGREDIENTS

6-ounce package semi-sweet chocolate
   pieces
2 tablespoons light or dark corn syrup
2 tablespoons butter
1½ teaspoons water

4 cups popped corn
1 cup shelled peanuts
½ cup shredded coconut (optional)
extra butter

1 • Boil water in the bottom of a double boiler. Remove the pan from the heat. In the top of the double boiler stir together one package of chocolate pieces, 2 tablespoons light or dark corn syrup, 2 tablespoons butter, and 1½ teaspoons water until chocolate melts.

2 • Pour the chocolate sauce over 4 cups popped corn, 1 cup shelled peanuts, and ½ cup shredded coconut in a large mixing bowl. Stir gently with a spoon until the sauce coats the corn mixture.

3 • Lightly grease a cookie sheet with butter. Drop spoonfuls of chocolate corn onto the sheet and refrigerate the clusters until the chocolate sets. You can also eat the chocolate popcorn and nuts while still warm.

BRAIDED CORNHUSK HOT PADS, MATS, AND BASKETS

MATERIALS

cornhusks
heavy-duty thread
needle
scissors

bowl of water
small bath towel
thumbtacks
small board

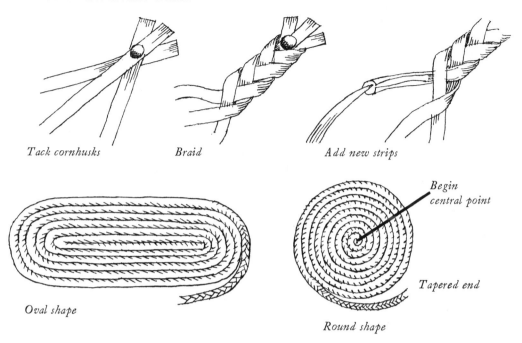

Tack cornhusks   *Braid*   *Add new strips*

Begin central point

Tapered end

Oval shape

Round shape

1 · Save a quantity of green husks from summer dinners of corn on the cob. String the green husks on a long length of strong thread with a needle. Hang the husks to dry for a week or more in an airy, shaded place until they become bleached and dry to the touch.

2 · Before braiding, soak the dry husks in a bowl of water. Keep the husks damp while you work. A small bath towel placed beneath the husks will absorb extra water and keep you dry.

3 · Tear the husks into long, narrow strips about ¾ to 1 inch wide. Take three strips of different lengths and tie them together in a knot or bind them together with heavy-duty thread. Tack the knotted end to a board and braid the husks (see illustrations above). Add new strips as each end shortens by folding each leaf lengthwise as you braid and pushing a small section of the leaf being added into the fold of the one that is almost used up. You can make yard-

long plaits, but be sure to add the new strips at different places so that the braid will not pull apart.

4 • Now you have lengths of braiding or plaiting from which you can make hot pads and mats by laying them flat side by side and sewing the coils together, or baskets by setting the braids on edge. Plaiting 1 inch wide and about 5 feet long will make a round mat 8 inches in diameter. You will need about 9 feet of ½-inch wide plaiting to make the same size mat.

5 • To make a round mat, coil a braid in a tight spiral about a central point. Use thumbtacks to fasten the spiral to the board in several places to hold the shape and sew the coiled rows together with a needle and heavy-duty thread. If you want to make an oval-shaped mat, lay the innermost braid in a straight line as long as your finger, then bend it back sharply in the opposite direction beyond the braid's beginning point and continue. Tack the spiral to the board to hold the shape and sew in place.

Basket

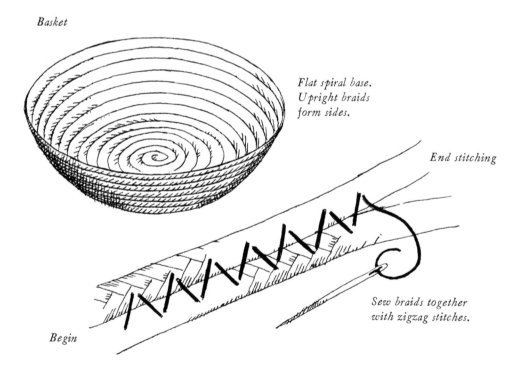

Flat spiral base.
Upright braids
form sides.

End stitching

Sew braids together
with zigzag stitches.

Begin

6 · To sew the braided coils together securely, begin at the center of the spiral mat and sew two rounds of braid together with zigzag stitches catching the outside edges of each braided coil. Then sew the second braided coil to the third. Continue until you sew every plaited coil to the one beside it. Work from the center to the outside edge of the mat.

7 · Give the mats a neat finish by cutting a few strips out of the end of the braid to make it gradually thinner. You then have a flat tapered end to sew.

8 · To make a basket, coil and sew a flat spiral mat the size you want to make the bottom. When the base of the basket is large enough, set the next round of plaiting *upright* (on edge) instead of flat. Sew the upright spiral to the base with zigzag stitches. Build up the basket's sides with additional spirals. Finish off by tapering the end of the braid.

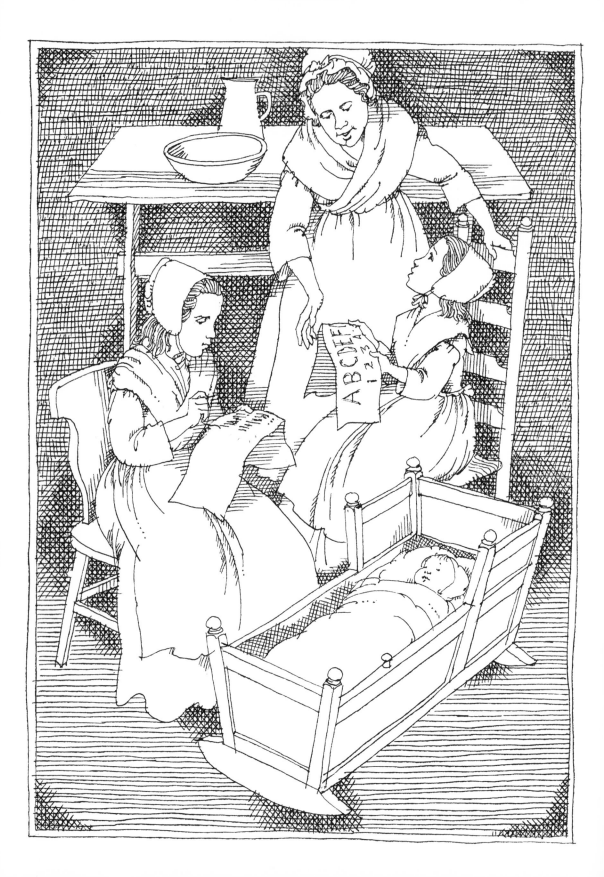

6

Samplers

Little girls in colonial America learned their ABCs at home on linen samplers instead of schoolroom blackboards. Mother cut a long, narrow piece of cloth about seven inches wide and three feet long for each daughter and drew the alphabet in large and small letters at the top. Underneath she put numbers from one to ten and added a short rhyme or verse.

Most girls dutifully followed Mother's instructions and labored long hours perfecting their stitches while they watched the sheep or rocked the baby. They learned cross-stitches, chain, satin, and outline stitches. Most stitched Bible verses, prayers, and poems like the one Mary Smith, age five, turned out: "Mary Smith is my name and with my nedel I wrought the same."

Older girls embroidered elaborate samplers with multiplication tables and pictures. They picked scenes of buildings, animals, people they knew, and biblical stories about Adam and Eve or Noah and the Ark. Those who excelled in needlework added bits of history and geography to their samplers. Elizabeth Ann Goldin embroidered a map of New York state on her sampler along with facts about its population and size. She even mentioned two American victories over the British before she finished.

Children less than five years old also worked on samplers. They had already knitted stockings and mittens so they were expected to master simple verses. Many embroidered:

> This is my Sampler,
> Here you see
> What care my Mother
> Took of me.

But sometimes a little girl showed her spunk. One child diligently labored over her sampler and stitched, "Patty Polk did this and she hated every stitch she did in it. She loves to read much more."

Samplers were old even in early America. They appeared in the England of Chaucer nearly three hundred years before the first English settlers came to America, and the royal account book of Elizabeth of York showed that a servant purchased sampler cloth for the English queen in 1502. The oldest existing sampler made in America belonged to Loara Standish, daughter of Myles Standish of Plymouth Colony. With home-dyed thread she worked intricate bands of flowers across the top and stitched, "Loara Standish is my name" in yellow and blue below.

You can create your own seventies version of a colonial sampler, and it need not be the drudgery Patty Polk thought it. Turn your fancywork into

Old-Fashioned Sampler Pattern

For canvas with 10 meshes per inch or burlap

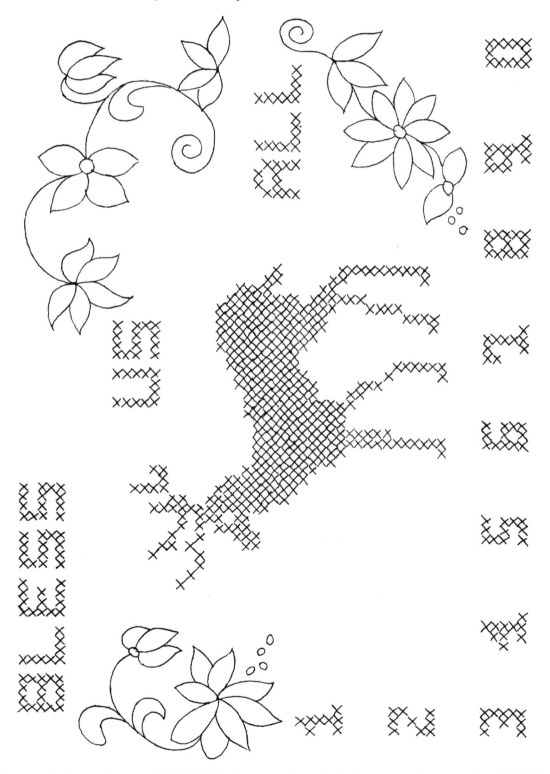

a picture, or wall hanging, or decorate a blouse. Just use the stitches shown on page 43. Practice them several times before you begin your sampler.

A SEVENTIES SAMPLER

MATERIALS

selection of colored embroidery floss or yarn
burlap or other cloth material with enough body to hold its shape
scissors
pencil

dressmaker's carbon paper (optional)
needle with a large eye
straight pins
For a wall hanging you will also need:
a wooden dowel or stick slightly longer than your hanging is wide

1 • Choose your embroidery floss or yarn and separate the strands. Make them thin enough to thread through your needle; two or three strands work best.

2 • Decide on a sampler. If you want to make a wall hanging or picture, be sure to select stiff material. Cut the material to the size you want. If there are frayed edges, turn under, pin, and sew them in place. You also can use embroidery stitches to fasten the edges.

3 • Choose a design or scene (keep it simple the first time) or try the sample shown (see illustration on p. 41) and draw it lightly on the material. If you select an intricate design, put a sheet of dressmaker's carbon or smudge-free carbon paper between the pattern and the material and trace.

4 • A variety of stitches gives the sampler texture and makes it interesting. Use more than one stitch (see illustrations on p. 43). Do not make knots in the ends of the thread or the finished piece will be lumpy. To start, draw the threaded needle through the material from back to front leaving a long end on the back.

Sampler Stitches

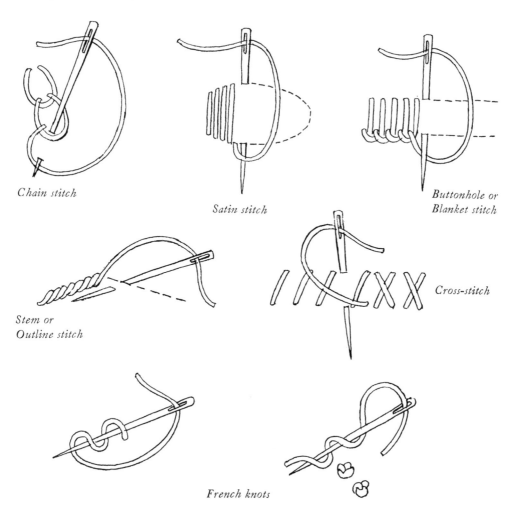

Chain stitch

Satin stitch

Buttonhole or Blanket stitch

Stem or Outline stitch

Cross-stitch

French knots

This end can be tucked under other threads and hidden when you finish. When your thread becomes too short to sew with, pull it under the stitches you have made and trim the end or pull it to the back and tuck it under other threads.

5 • The dowel or stick will make a hanger. Simply fold the top of the material over the stick and sew the two layers together.

6 • You can also display your fancy work on a blouse; just follow directions 1 through 4. Collars, lapels, shirt yokes, pockets, and cuffs are good places to embroider because they have a double thickness and you can hide loose ends between them.

Many colonial women shared "friendship quilts" with friends and relatives. Each person wrote his or her name in a quilt block and embroidered it. After a woman sewed all the blocks together and quilted her cover, she possessed a beautiful reminder of all her friends. You can remember your friends with this friendship pillow.

FRIENDSHIP PILLOW

MATERIALS

two pieces of cloth	*embroidery floss or yarn*
ruler	*straight pins*
chalk	*thread*
scissors	*needle with a large eye*
waterproof ink pen	*foam pillow stuffing or old rags*

1 • Choose the pillow size you want, measure the cloth and mark the proper size in chalk, and cut two pieces of cloth that size, allowing an extra inch on all sides for seams. Have your friends sign their names in waterproof ink on one or both sides of the pillow and embroider them. Don't embroider too close to the edges or you will sew the design into the seams.

2 • When finished, pin the two layers of material together with the right sides

facing and sew four corners and three sides. Turn the right sides out, fill the pillow with stuffing, and sew the fourth side closed.

3 · Or embroider your friends' signatures in each block of the patchwork pillow described in the chapter on the Quilting Bee. For either pillow, you might use several different colored yarns to provide a gay contrast with the background.

7

Rhythm of the Wheel

The buzz and hum of spinning wheels rose and fell, high and low. Almost every woman in early America, married or single, was a spinster, a spinner of yarn. Some even had two spinning wheels. They stood and hand-pushed the big "high" wheel to spin wool and sat and foot-pedaled a small wheel to spin flax. As they deftly pulled the strands and watched the bobbin fatten, spinners planned the coverlets, blankets, and breeches their yarn would make.

In the spring before they turned the animals out to pasture, men and boys carefully sheared the sheep and carried the oily, matted wool to the house where everyone picked cockleburs, sticks, and leaves from the tangled fleece.

Then they washed the dirty wool and carded or straightened the fibers between two wooden paddles shaped like stable currycombs and rolled the smooth strands into balls ready for spinning.

Pioneer women also dyed the yarn and thread they spun. A favorite color was blue, in all shades, made from the indigo plant. They pressed goldenrod flowers to make a yellow dye and mixed it with indigo blue. Together the dyes made a beautiful green. Boiled sassafras bark made pink and orange, and purple juice from iris petals gave a soft violet. Women took great pride in the colors they created, and spent hours under the trees tending the pots of boiling dye to get just the right shade for a new dress or jacket.

When women finished spinning and dyeing the wool and flax, they wove it into lengths of cloth. Some households had no loom, so spinsters carried their yarn to the village weaver. Children loved to watch the weavers work and begged for bits of colored yarn to braid or weave. They used small lap looms only a few inches wide to make shoestrings, hairlaces, hatbands, and glove ties. Boys turned out suspenders and garters to hold up their trousers and hose.

Over and under, over and under. *Thwack, thwack, thwack,* went the weaver's loom. As he swiftly threw the shuttle back and forth across the loom, the weaver made many patterns—over-shot, double-shot, summer and winter weave. A weaver kept the directions for these patterns on sheets of paper called "drafts" and exchanged favorite ones with other weavers the way good cooks trade recipes.

When the American Revolution came, spinsters joined the rebels and boycotted English tea and cloth. They proudly dressed their families in scratchy homespun clothes and wove blankets and coats for the soldiers. The British soon called George Washington's troops the "Homespuns" because every man who volunteered for eight months' service received a coat spun by his countrywomen as bounty.

WEAVING

Making the Loom

MATERIALS

*old picture frame or four 1-inch-thick   ruler
   pieces of wood at least 12 inches long   scissors*
nails (about 24)   strong string
hammer

1 • Hammer nails across the two short ends of an old picture frame. Place the nails at equal intervals, about ½ inch apart. At least ¼ inch of nail should stick up above the frame.

2 • If you do not have a picture frame, make a loom with four 1-inch-thick pieces of wood 12 inches long. Lay two lengths parallel and 10 inches apart. Balance the two remaining lengths of wood on top of the two parallel pieces, one at each end, to make a square. Nail the four corners. Hammer nails ½ inch apart on two opposite sides as explained above. Now you have a square frame for your loom. (See illustration on p. 50.)

3 • Tie a length of heavy string to one corner nail. Pull the string across the loom and around the first *two* nails on the opposite side. Continue drawing the string back and forth across the loom and around every two nails until you reach the last nail. Tie a knot and cut off the extra string. (See illustration on p. 50.) This is the warp of your loom.

Making the Loom

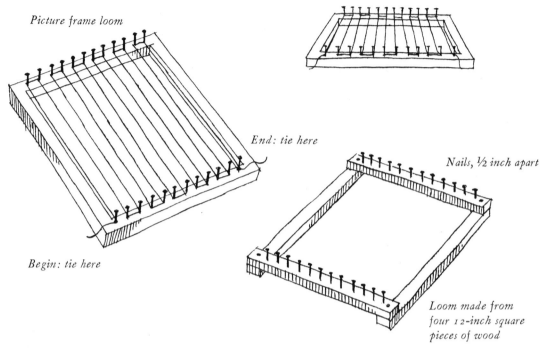

Picture frame loom

End: tie here

Nails, ½ inch apart

Begin: tie here

Loom made from four 12-inch square pieces of wood

Lay loom flat on worktable to weave

Weaving

MATERIALS

loom

weaving materials—straw, grasses, bark, reeds, and sticks or different colored yarns

large pan of water to soak dried materials

scissors

ruler

needle

heavy-duty thread

stick or wooden dowel slightly longer than the width of your woven material (for a wall hanging)

1 • Cut your weaving material into lengths approximately 4 inches longer

than the width of your loom. If some pieces are short, overlap the ends of two or more lengths to fit across the loom.

2 • Weave your material this way: Go over the first string and under the next. Continue *over one, under one* until you reach the opposite side of the loom. Push this first row close to the nails. Let about two inches of weaving material hang over the edge of the frame on both sides.

3 • Weave other lengths through one at a time. Each time go *over* the string you went *under* before and go *under* the string you went *over* before.

4 • Fill the loom with weaving material. Be sure to keep the pieces close together. Try different patterns by skipping strings, leaving open spaces, using different materials and weaving them together—yarn with grass, sticks with leaves. Be sure to soak the dried materials such as grasses and reeds in a large pan of water to make them soft and pliable.

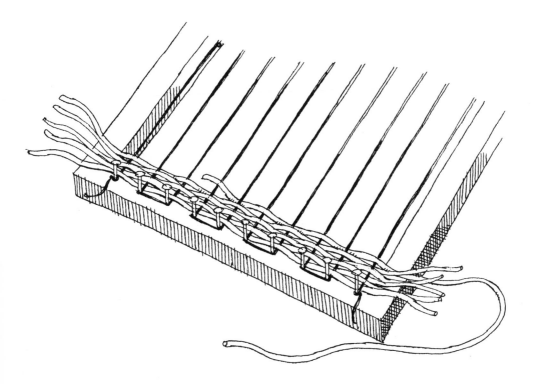

5 • When you finish filling the loom with materials, slowly lift the weaving off the nails. (Add more lengths of weaving material to the ends, if necessary, to make the weaving tight and to give it more strength.)

6 • Trim uneven ends and sew along both edges to keep the weaving in place. The finished woven mat will be large enough for a table mat, a small doll blanket, or dresser scarf. Sew several mats together to make large mats.

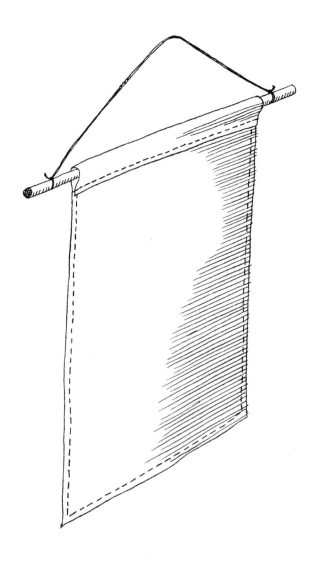

7 · To make a wall hanging, cut a stick or dowel slightly longer than the width of your woven material. Lap the loose ends of one side over the dowel and sew through the double thickness close to the dowel. This will be your hanger.

8

Candlelight

Candles lighted the darkness when settlers first came to America. The town watchman carried a candle lantern when he made his rounds, and travelers on the roads depended on a candle's light to see.

Families at home treasured their tallow tapers and burned them only when necessary. Women often used the light from the fireplace to sew, and men, rather than waste a candle, took a torch to the barn when they fed the animals.

Until peddlers sold tin candle molds, the colonists spun their own candle wicks and dipped them by hand into warm tallow made from animal fat. As each tallow layer cooled, they dipped the wicks again and again, and the candles grew fatter and fatter. Then they hung them to cool. When home-makers finally owned candle molds, they could make six, eight, twelve, or twenty-four tapers at one time. They merely hung the wicks in the molds and filled each hole with tallow.

Women hoarded fat all year for candles. They saved every table scrap and piece of suet. Then they spent two or three days boiling down the fat into tallow. No one wanted to be inside while it cooked. The house smelled of rancid fat, and the children preferred to play outside even in freezing weather.

Some colonists made candles from beeswax, but everyone liked the bay-berry wax candles best. They burned slowly and gave a clear, steady flame. Women often lighted a bayberry candle just before company came and then snuffed it out when they arrived. The lingering smoke filled the room with a sweet perfume.

Every autumn the children picked the tiny gray-green bayberries that grew on bushes near the sea. It took thousands of berries to make enough wax for one candle, yet some households collected berries to make fragrant soap and sealing wax as well. Many communities passed laws to protect their valuable berry crop. Anyone who picked unripe berries paid a fine of fifteen shillings.

TIN CAN CANDLES

MATERIALS

empty round tin can to mold the candle (tuna fish, soup, or juice cans will do)

newspapers
stubs from used candles or paraffin (about 1 pound)

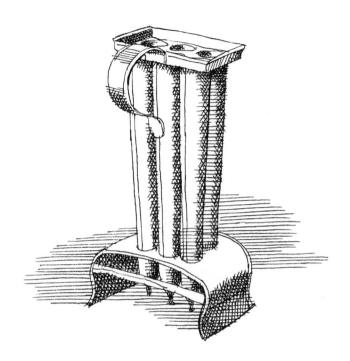

cooking or mineral oil

small nail

cotton candle wicking or a length of
  medium-weight white string 4 inches
  longer than the tin can mold

pencil

string-wick solution—1 cup water,
  1 tablespoon salt, 2 tablespoons
  borax

a large tin can (a 1- or 2-pound coffee
  can) set in a large pan of water

kitchen tongs

old crayons

old long-handled spoon or stick

cup of cold water

sharp knife

soft rag

scissors

1 • Wash the inside of the tin can mold with soap and water. Rub the inside
with oil.

2 • Tie the nail to the end of the cotton candle wicking and drop it into the
center of the can. Tie the loose end around the center of the pencil and rest the
pencil across the top of the can. Keep the wicking straight by wrapping extra

wicking around the pencil. This will be your wick. If you use string, first soak it in a solution of 1 cup water, 1 tablespoon salt, and 2 tablespoons borax, and hang the string to dry. This helps ordinary string absorb enough wax to burn well. Put the can on several layers of newspaper to catch spills.

3 • Break the paraffin into pieces and put the pieces into a large coffee can. Pinch the top edge of the can together to make a pouring spout. If you are using old candles, add them as well. Stores usually sell paraffin in pound blocks. One pound of paraffin will fill several small cans.

4 • Place the coffee can in a large pan containing a small amount of water. Simmer the water to melt the paraffin slowly. Do not let it boil. If you use candle stubs, the old wicks will float to the top. Pick them out with kitchen tongs.

5 • After the paraffin melts completely, take the can off the stove, and add pieces of old crayons to the paraffin. (Be sure to remove the paper.) Stir the paraffin with an old spoon or clean stick. Test the color by pouring a little paraffin into a cup of cold water. The color will look lighter than it will in the finished candle, but you can see the tone and add more crayon if you choose. Reheat the wax, but do not let it boil. Be careful handling the paraffin—it will stay hot for a long time.

6 • Slowly pour the melted paraffin into the tin can mold. Let the paraffin flow down the sides of the mold so air bubbles will not form. Fill the mold about three-quarters full, but save at least ½ cup of paraffin to fill the cavity that will be made when the candle shrinks and sinks in the middle as it hardens. Set the can aside until the wax hardens and cools.

7 • Reheat the leftover paraffin and fill the sunken area in the center when the candle is cool, but fill only to the top of the first pouring. If the hot paraffin runs over and down the sides between the candle and the mold, it ruins the smooth surface and makes the candle hard to remove.

8 · To make striped candles of more than one color, let each colored layer harden before you pour the next. It takes several hours for each stripe to set. Experiment—try pouring fat stripes and thin stripes to make each candle different.

9 · Leave the finished candle at room temperature for about eight hours or overnight. Then turn the can upside down to remove the candle. Tap the sides if it sticks or quickly dip the mold up to the rim in hot water. Remove the seam line with a sharp knife, then polish the sides with a soft rag and clip the wick with scissors about one inch from the top of the candle. Put the candle in a cool place to cure for five or six days before burning.

9

Rugmaking

No child in the New World ever walked on the family's tapestry rugs. Proud owners hung them on walls or covered tables with them, but they never put them under foot. Imported from Holland or the Near East, they were too valuable to use as dirt catchers.

Most of the first homes in America had sand or dirt floors. Every day the colonists raked up the mud, kitchen grease, and candle wax that had been accidentally dropped. Then they wet the dry sand or dirt to keep the dust down and made it smooth with a broom or turkey wing. When a wood floor was finally laid, women wove rush mats and later rag rugs like cloth on looms.

In the evenings or on rainy days women emptied a rag bag on the table, sorted, cut, and sewed the cloth scraps into long, narrow strips. Sometimes children helped and rolled the strips into balls. When they collected enough strips, a weaver wove the lengths of cloth into rugs. One large ball made about one yard of carpet.

Women also braided rugs. They first twined strips of cloth into long braided strands and then coiled them into round or oval carpets. Little girls saved the prettiest, brightest cloth scraps for throw rugs by the fire. Old, worn carpets became foot wipers and soft blankets for new spring lambs.

Scandinavian colonists made hooked or "drawn-in" rugs with their rags. They stretched a cloth canvas riddled with small holes on a wooden frame and, with long needles, poked rag strips into the openings. Wealthy women used wool yarn instead of rags and hooked pictures of colorful flowers, family pets, and country scenes.

Well-to-do people also hired traveling painters to decorate their floorboards. The painter laid a solid coat of paint made with egg whites or skim milk on the floor and then spattered many colors over it. Some people preferred a stenciled floor design with wide borders, flowers, fruit, and trailing vines or flying eagles. Whenever the itinerant painter traveled by, children scurried to meet him. He knew all the latest news and gossip for miles around.

A BRAIDED RUG

MATERIALS

cloth in assorted colors
scissors
a bodkin needle or other long needle
carpet thread

pillow or board to secure cloth strip
ends while braiding
thumbtacks or safety pins
piece of cardboard to hold braid

1 • Choose cloth that is approximately the same weight. If you buy new material, be sure to wash it to remove sizing and reduce shrinkage before you begin.

2 • Tear or cut the cloth lengthwise into 2-inch-wide strips. Trim the ends diagonally and sew the strips together end to end with right sides facing.

3 • Select three long strips, lay them side by side, and sew them together at one end. Pin or tack the sewn end to a pillow or board. To braid, fold the left strip over the middle strip and the right strip over the left. Roll the rough edges toward the center to avoid raw edges showing and keep the plaiting tight and even. As an end grows short, sew on another cloth strip and continue braiding. Fold the braided cloth strips around a piece of cardboard until you have enough braid to begin coiling it into a rug. (See illustrations on p. 64.)

4 • Thread the needle, but do not make the thread too long or it will tangle. Tie a large knot in the end. Holding the braid flat, coil the sewn end into a tight circle. Pin with a safety pin, if necessary, to hold it in place. Continue to hold the rug flat—working on a table will help—and sew the coil together firmly. Bring the thread through the outside edge of the braid already coiled, into and through the outside edge of the braid you add. Keep coiling and sewing the braid this way with zigzag stitches. Knot the thread tightly when you come to the end. Use the safety pins to hold the coil in place until you sew it down. Do not pull the braid too tightly as you coil it or the rug will pucker.

Braided Rug

Step 3

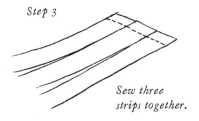

Sew three strips together.

Step 3

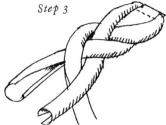

Braid and roll rough edges toward center.

Step 4

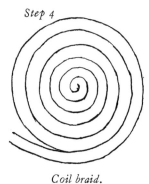

Coil braid.

Step 4

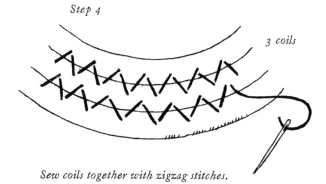

3 coils

Sew coils together with zigzag stitches.

5 • You can sew additional cloth strips to the ends as you coil the rug and then braid them to make the rug size that you want. Use a small rug as a table placemat, a throw rug by the door, or beside your bed. Keep your first rug small and easy to do.

A HOOKED RUG PICTURE

MATERIALS

ready-made rug canvas or a piece of burlap, 13 x 13 inches

scissors

masking tape or needle and thread

waterproof pen to mark design
tracing paper
ruler
crochet hook
strip of cardboard 6 inches long and
    ⅜ inch wide

assorted colored yarn (not too thick):
    one 2-oz. skein for color in the de-
    sign; one 4-oz. skein for the back-
    ground
dressmaker's carbon paper
pencil

1 • Buy ready-made rug canvas or use a piece of burlap. With scissors cut it into a 13 x 13-inch square and sew or tape the frayed edges so the burlap will not unravel. Draw a margin 1½ inches from the edge on all sides. Select burlap that is the same color as the background color of your design.

2 • Draw a simple pattern on the canvas or follow the sample design shown on page 66. Trace the design and transfer it to the burlap by placing a piece of dressmaker's carbon paper between the tracing paper and the burlap, with the carbon side toward the burlap. Trace firmly once again over the design. Be sure to place the design in the center of the canvas. Remove the carbon paper and the tracing paper, and mark the color for each area in the design on the canvas.

3 • On an extra piece of canvas, practice your hooking before you begin the picture. Cut a piece of yarn about 20 inches long. Hold the canvas in your lap or on a table. If you are right-handed, use your left hand to press the yarn against the back of the canvas. With your right hand, push the tip of the crochet hook from the front of the canvas through a hole, catch the yarn, and draw a loop back through the hole and make it stand up about ⅜ inch. Use your cardboard strip as a guide to keep all your loops even. Skip two or three holes and repeat pulling a loop through the canvas. If you are left-handed, hold the canvas in your right hand and the hook in the left.

4 • When you are ready to hook your picture, outline the design first with loops and then fill it in. When the yarn becomes too short to hook, tuck the loose end

Hooked Rug Picture Design

yellow

green

red

black

green

red

blue

green

red

blue

black

green

red

yellow

red

Cut material 13 x 13 inches and center design.

red

under threads on the back of the canvas. Avoid making knots in the yarn. Select or make a frame without glass for your picture. You can also sew several squares together and make a rug.

10

Shades of the Past

Peddlers trudged America's back roads long before stores carrying civilization's wares reached the rural countryside. These traveling men sallied forth with pushcarts, pack-a-back sacks and small wagons laden with seeds and seedlings, needles and nails, pots and pans. All were welcome, but children saved their heartiest hurrahs for the shademaker.

The shademaker, or, as some people called him, the shadowmaker or profilist, made portraits. A person sat between a lighted candle and a piece of translucent paper attached to a glass-and-frame contraption while the shademaker carefully traced the subject's shadowed profile on the paper. Then the shadowmaker reduced the profile to the appropriate size with a device called a pantograph, inked in the tracings, mounted, and framed it. Most portraits were black on a white background, but sometimes the profilist selected an ink or fabric in sepia, green, or deep red. Unlike an oil portrait painted by a traveling artist, a shadowgraph seldom flattered people. It showed every cowlick, crooked nose, and sagging chin.

People also called shadowgraphs "silhouettes" after the penny-pinching French Minister of Finance, Etienne Silhouette. Like Etienne, who practiced thrift instead of extravagance, the shademaker substituted the inexpensive silhouette for the costly oil portrait. Even amateurs tried their hand. Nelly Custis, granddaughter of George and Martha Washington, observed their shadows on the walls of their Mount Vernon home in the early evening hours and snipped her grandparents' silhouettes.

Master silhouettists dispensed with machines and cut profiles freehand. They set up shops in the large eastern seaboard towns and advertised their skill. Expert artists rarely produced life-size profiles. Most silhouettes measured less than three inches in height. Some of the finest were less than half an inch high and were mounted in lockets, brooches, and snuffbox lids.

Silhouettists such as William Henry Brown cut elaborate scenes of American life as well as family portraits. Brown's detailed shades pictured sailing ships, railway trains, and fire companies. He made one twenty-five-foot long silhouette of the St. Louis Fire Brigade complete with engines, hose carriages, and fire fighters.

SILHOUETTES

MATERIALS

masking tape   *sharp lead pencil*

2 large sheets of smooth, lightweight   *scissors*
paper (2 different colors, one light   *white, water-soluble glue*
  and one dark)   *picture frame or colored mat made with*
blank wall with a smooth surface   *poster cardboard*
flashlight

1 · Tape a large sheet of smooth, lightweight paper on a smooth, blank wall. Any color paper will do. It should be large enough to contain a profile the size you want.

2 · Find someone to sit for you and place him between the paper and a flashlight. You can rest the flashlight on a table, propping it up with books if necessary. Move the sitter or the illuminated flashlight forward or backward to adjust the size of the silhouette to fit your paper. Turn the sitter's head until his profile shadow is sharp and clear.

3 · Do your tracing at night with only one light source—your flashlight. (An unshaded light bulb also works.) Carefully trace around the shadowed profile. Don't forget to include wisps of hair, forehead wrinkles, and the neckline. They make an accurate portrait of your subject.

4 · Cut out the silhouette and glue it to a second sheet of paper, or hollow-cut the silhouette by cutting out all the paper *within* the tracings. Mount the hollow-cut *over* the second sheet of paper.

5 · Select a traditional picture frame or make a colored mat or frame with poster cardboard. Use your silhouette on stationery or greeting cards. Try silhouettes of your family and friends, even your dog—if he or she will hold still!

11

Papyrotamia

Paper was priceless in early America so every piece was saved and hoarded in a special cupboard drawer. On important occasions a well-wisher would carefully choose a sheet of paper, fold it, and cut out a beautiful design in honor of someone's birthday, anniversary, or wedding.

Sometimes a clever and patient person cut birds and deer, flowers and valentines. Others loved intricate patterns with lots of curlicues and swirls. At Christmas many families made delicate paper chains for their holiday tree.

Some people simply called this art paper cutting, but others used the high-sounding name "papyrotamia." Women with artistic talent and steady hands spent long hours planning a paper cutting, tracing a design, and then trimming away the excess paper to reveal landscapes and street scenes, flower bouquets and baskets of fruit. They mounted their best work on paper and framed and glazed it. Sometimes they willed a favorite cutting to a friend.

Cutting paper pictures is an ancient art. Some cuttings hang as works of art in museums. Asian and European monarchs cut paper as a royal pastime, and a craft guild in sixteenth-century Turkey exhibited before the sultan of Constantinople a huge castle and garden carved from multicolored papers. European painters cut folded paper into stencils for painting borders around church paintings and choir stalls. Rural artists used paper stencils to decorate family chests, furniture, and household utensils.

By the eighteenth century, paper cutting adorned religious texts, love notes, and legal documents. Booksellers designed paper cuttings for covers and seals. One Boston woman visually recorded for her ancestors the entire family home and farm in papyrotamia pictures.

Papyrotamia cut from colored paper and mounted on heavy paper or cardboard makes beautiful wall decorations and pictures. Small paper cuttings become unusual greeting cards for Christmas and other holidays. Linked together they form colored paper chains for party decorations or Christmas trees.

First decide on what you want to make—paper pictures, chains, or greeting cards—and choose the appropriate weight of paper. Smooth, thin paper works best for cards and designs with intricate detail. Tissue, construction, or foil papers make elegant chains.

Paper Cuttings

MATERIALS

paper (different weights and colors)
sharp pencil
large scissors to cut large areas and
small scissors with very sharp tips
to cut details

mounting paper for background
white, water-soluble glue
masking tape
stapler and staples or strong string

WALL DECORATIONS, PICTURES, AND CARDS

1 • Begin with a simple design, something like paper cutting #1 on page 76 to get started. Fold the paper in half. Lightly draw your design—a bird, flower, or tree—on the paper with a pencil. Keep the fold in the center of your design. Then carefully cut out your picture. Use small, pointed scissors to cut details. If you hold the scissors motionless and *move the paper,* you can cut intricate shapes without difficulty. Then open the fold and you have your first paper cutting .

2 • To preserve your cutting, glue it to another sheet of paper or cardboard in a contrasting color. Use a small piece of paper to apply the glue to large areas, corners, and edges. Not every inch of paper needs glue. Glue the middle first and then the corners.

3 • You can make more complicated designs by folding the paper more than once. First fold a sheet of paper in half and then in half again so there are four layers. Tape the loose edges and corners together to hold the layers in place. Lightly draw the design on the paper using the two folds as the base and center of your design. Follow directions for paper cutting #2 on page 77 to see how

Paper Cutting #1

fold

Fold paper in half.
Draw design with
fold in the center.
Cut out design and unfold.

Mount paper cutting on
another sheet of paper.

Paper Cutting #2

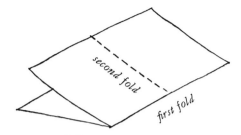

Fold paper in half.

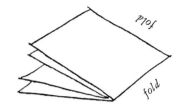

Fold paper in half again.

Draw design using folds as base and center of the pattern.

fold (center of design)

fold (base of design)

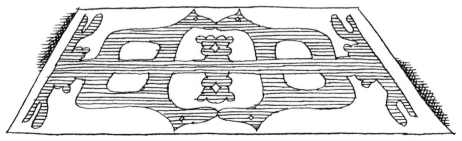

Unfold cutting. Glue to another sheet of paper in a contrasting color.

Paper Cutting #3

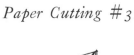

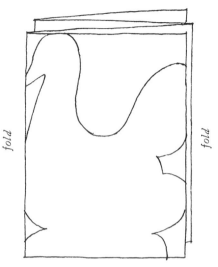

*Fold strip of paper in
many accordion pleats.*

fold

fold

Draw design.

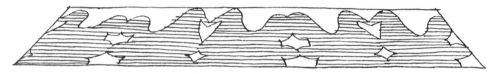

Snowflake #4

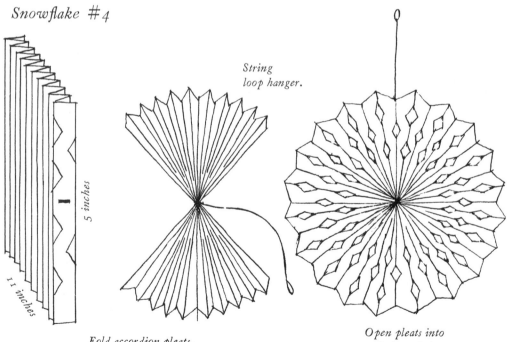

5 inches

11 inches

*String
loop hanger.*

*Fold accordion pleats.
Staple center.
Make cuts along both sides.*

*Open pleats into
a circle and glue.*

to do it. Cut out your design, open the folds, and you have a four-figured de-sign. Experiment.

PAPER CHAINS AND SNOWFLAKES

1 • To make paper chains for party decorations or Christmas trees, fold a long, narrow strip of paper many times in accordion pleats. To do this, fold the end of the paper over at least two inches. Turn the paper over and make a fold on the same end, the same width as the first fold but in the *opposite* direction. Continue turning and folding the same end of the paper until the entire length is evenly pleated.

Draw a figure—a bell, bird, or doll—and cut out the shape. Make sure you don't cut completely through the folds on either side. Unfold the paper and you have a row of connected figures. To make longer chains, glue or tape additional lengths together. (See paper cutting #3 on p. 78.)

2 • For a Christmas tree or party, make delicate paper snowflakes. Fold a sheet of white paper 5 inches wide and 11 inches long into half-inch wide accordion pleats. Staple or tie the paper with strong string in the center. Make cuts along both sides of the folded strip. (See paper cutting #4 on p. 78.) Open the snow-flake and spread the pleats into a circle. Hold the two halves of the circle in place with glue. Attach a loop of string or white thread between the pleats as you glue the circle, so you can hang the snowflake. Make smaller snowflakes with strips of paper 3 and 4 inches wide.

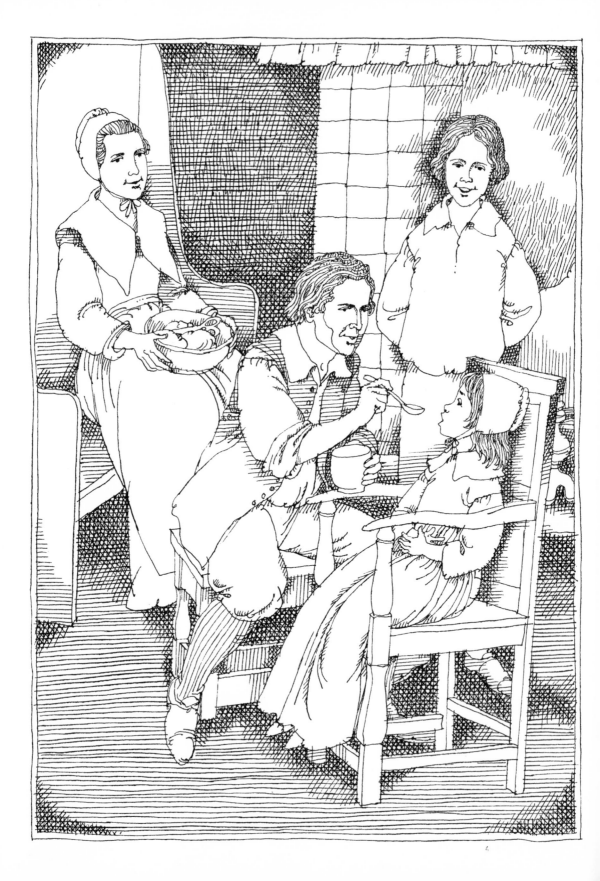

12

Sassafras Tea in the Spring

"One herb for the head, another for the back, a third for the chest, and one for when you don't feel so good," colonial women often said. That was their prescription for good health and long life. No pills or patent medicines for them. They depended on the herbs, roots, leaves, and bark that grew in "nature's medicine cabinet" to cure their families' ills.

Every morning before the sun grew hot, colonists went to the garden with rakes and hoes to cultivate a profusion of medicinal herbs—lad's love, tansy, sarsaparilla, and spearmint. When someone had a fever, the proper herbs were collected, blended, and boiled into a healthful broth. Children with sore throats gargled thyme and honey, and those with upset stomachs from overeating downed sarsaparilla or peppermint tea.

Self-taught folk doctors with homegrown remedies administered their medicines with the force and zeal of true physicians. Knowledgeable practitioners prescribed a spearmint drink for toothaches and catnip for colicky babies, covered burns with witch-hazel salve, and applied a sunflower-seed solution to sore eyes. Everyone ate onions to clot the blood and drank sassafras-root tea in the spring to "thin the blood."

Many settlers also hunted in the woods for the Indian turnip called jack-in-the-pulpit. When its berries turned bright red, they pulled up the bulbs, peeled, and hung them on long cane poles across the rafters in the kitchen. There the bulbs dried along with leaf tobacco, smartweed, and mullein until someone needed them. In winter women grated a jack-in-the-pulpit bulb into milk, hot water, and sugar to fight grippe and made excellent poultices for injured arms and legs with smartweed and mullein leaves.

Garden herbs kept the family healthy, but colonists found other uses for them. They gathered herbal flowers and leaves along with garden spices and put them into scented sachets. Heaped in baskets or placed in cupboards, fragrant pomander balls hid the unpleasant cooking odors and the strong smell of woodsmoke and tobacco. Women often tucked a spiced pomander or sachet into a handkerchief when they traveled to town so they could sniff its sweet, spicy scent instead of foul street smells.

POMANDER BALLS

MATERIALS

fork or toothpick
jar of whole cloves

dish of powdered cinnamon or allspice
cheesecloth

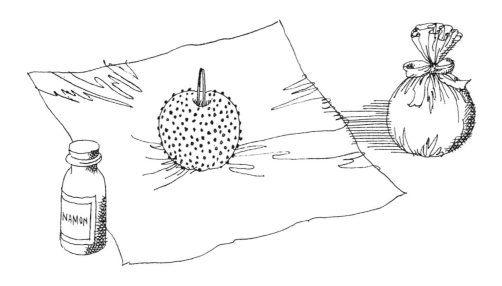

firm, ripe fruit—apples, oranges, lemons or limes, even crab apples or
   mock-orange fruit
wire hairpins

string
scissors
ribbon or yarn

1 • Select firm, ripe fruit and prick dozens of tiny holes in the skin with a fork
or toothpick. Keep the holes close together and work in small areas. Gently push
a whole clove into each hole. Cover the entire surface with cloves.

2 • Push the tips of a wire hairpin into the stem end of the fruit. Roll the fruit
in cinnamon or allspice and place it in the center of a large square of cheesecloth.
The cheesecloth holds the spice around the fruit until the spicy odors and fruit
juices mingle and mellow. Draw the corners of cheesecloth together and twist
around the hairpin. Tie the corners tightly with a length of string and cut off
the loose ends, and then tie a bow with colored ribbon or yarn around the
string.

3 • Let the fruit dry in a cool, dark place (a closet where air circulates) for
about two to three weeks or until the fruit is hard. Prick tiny holes in the cheesecloth and place the pomander in a dresser drawer or hang it in your closet. You

also can remove the wrapping and give the spicy ball as a gift to friends or hang it on your Christmas tree.

4 • If you want to keep your dried pomander fresh to give as a gift later, put it in a plastic sandwich bag and tie the ends. Place it in a box, plastic container, or can and seal the edges with tape.

SACHETS

MATERIALS

flower petals from roses and violets, or
   leaves of rose geranium and lemon
   verbena plants
cake rack
mixing bowl
spoon
powdered spices—cinnamon, cloves,
   and allspice
scissors or pinking shears
4-inch diameter circles of thin cloth
   such as batiste or organdie
strong thread
narrow ribbon or yarn

1 • You can make sachets of single or mixed flower and spice scents. Collect the petals or leaves and spread them to dry on a wire cake rack. Allow them to dry until you can crumble them between your fingers. (This will take about three or four days to two weeks.)

2 • Crumble the petals and leaves into a bowl and stir in powdered spices— cinnamon, cloves, and allspice. Use enough spice to dust the mixture thoroughly.

3 • Cut circles 4 inches in diameter of thin cloth. You can use pinking shears to give the sachets a delicate, lacy edge. Put one or two spoonfuls of the flower and spice mixture in the center of the circle. Draw the edges together, twist,

and tie them tightly with strong thread. Cover the thread with a colorful piece of ribbon or yarn.

AN HERB GARDEN

MATERIALS

herb seeds—parsley, sage, chives, and dill

egg cartons (paper cartons work best)

nail

small pebbles

soil

small container filled with water

containers for herb seedlings—clay pots; plastic ice cream, cottage cheese, or margarine containers; or styrofoam cups or empty milk cartons

1 • Select your herbs and carefully read the planting directions on the packets.

2 • Collect several egg cartons and with a nail punch two or three drainage holes in the bottom of each egg slot. Put a few tiny pebbles in the bottom, add a little soil, and three or four seeds to each slot. Sprinkle just enough dirt over the seeds to cover them—usually about one-quarter inch of soil.

3 • Do not let the soil dry out. Place the carton in a light or sunny window away from cold air drafts. The soil must be kept warm and moist so check it every day. Keep a small container filled with water near the plants. The water will evaporate and keep the air moist.

4 • When the seedlings grow two or three inches high, they are ready to be transplanted to larger containers. Clay pots are best, but plastic ice cream, cottage cheese, or margarine containers will work. You can also use styrofoam cups or empty milk cartons cut down to six or eight inches high. Punch drainage holes in the bottom with a nail, add a layer of small pebbles, and a layer of dirt.

5 • Break the egg carton into sections, remove the seedlings with a dirt ball around the roots, and gently put the seedlings and the dirt ball in the center of the larger container and fill it with dirt.

6 • Keep the soil moist but not soggy. Push a toothpick into the soil; if it comes out clean, the herbs probably need water. Add a few broken eggshells, coffee grounds, or used tea leaves to the soil. Plants need food, too.

7 • If you regularly pick the herbs, the plants will continue to grow indefinitely. When the roots begin to show through the drainage hole, it's time to transfer the plant to a larger container.

DRYING HERBS

MATERIALS

leafy herbs
cake rack
small containers with tight-fitting lids
  such as baby food jars or vitamin
  bottles

sheet of paper
marking pen
tape

1 • Pick your leafy herbs when the plants' flowers begin to open. The leaves have their strongest aroma then. Pinch off entire stalks, but leave at least 2 or 3 inches so new shoots will grow. Wash the stalks in cool water and shake off excess moisture.

2 • Tear off the leaves from the stems and spread them to dry in a single layer on a wire cake rack. Allow air to circulate above and below the rack. Stir the leaves once a day. The leaves are dry if they crumble when pressed between your fingers. (This will take about four days to two weeks.)

3 • Put the dried, crumbled, or whole leaves into airtight containers and store them in a dark place. Make labels for the jars. Write the herb's name on each jar so you will know the contents. Soon you will know an herb by its aroma and you won't need a label to tell chive from sage.

4 • Sprinkle your dried herbs on meat and vegetables before roasting or baking; add them to simmering soups and stews for your own special flavoring. You also can mix dried herbs in your sachets and pomanders, or bottle them in pretty containers to give as gifts.

13

Everlasting Bouquets

Frontier colonists worked hard sewing and cooking, weaving and washing, harvesting and hunting, but each spring, on the first fine day, everyone laid other work aside and spent the entire day putting in a garden. They planted row after row of turnips and parsnips, pumpkin and squash for hungry mouths to eat, but somehow these hardy pioneers always saved space for a patch of flowers. Flowers, some said, were God's breath upon the world.

Many settlers knew how to make their flowers bloom all year. They followed the example of early botanist Peter Kalm, who, without a camera to record his botanical specimens, pressed leaves, flowers, and sometimes entire plants—roots, seeds, and pods—between sheets of weighted paper. Kalm dissected and studied his finds, but colonial homemakers mounted and framed their blossoms and hung them on the cabin walls just to be looked at and admired.

Women picked garden flowers to decorate their homes. They tied them in bunches and hung them upside down from the cabin rafters to dry— bunches of statice, salvia, cockscomb, and iris. At harvest they added sheaves of wheat and oats, corn and cane tassels, and stalks of plumed grasses.

In the fall children gathered sycamore balls and sweet gum stars and brought home milkweed and mullein which dried naturally outdoors. Other plants dried best buried in sand or meal, so housewives kept boxes filled with these blossoms in cool corners of the house. When the fragile flowers and delicate leaves dried sufficiently, containers filled with sand were used to anchor charming flower arrangements.

Dried flowers served as air fresheners as well as colorful bouquets. In the seventeenth and eighteenth centuries, English families spiced dried flower petals with expensive oils, perfumes, and sandalwood chips and put them in tight containers. When they opened the lid, sweet-smelling scents filled the room and replaced the stale odors of close quarters. Colonial women never owned costly oils, but they substituted kitchen herbs and spices. Allowed to mellow, their inexpensive potpourris lasted for months.

PRESSED FLOWER FANCIES

MATERIALS

garden or wild flowers, leaves, and
  grasses
can of water to carry picked flowers
newspapers

name tags for flowers
white, water-soluble glue
loose-leaf school notebooks or spirals
  (to make herbarium books)

heavy books or bricks
to quick-dry flowers: waxed paper,
* newspaper, iron*
mounting paper for background—
* colored construction or plain white*
* paper*

toothpicks
scissors
pencil
ruler
picture frame (optional)
plastic wrap (optional)

1 • Pick garden or wild flowers and put them in a can of water so they won't wilt before you press them. Choose small flowers, little leaves, and grasses. Single petals and grass stems work too. Remember—never pick a flower if it is the only one.

2 • Dry a large number of flowers so you will have a selection. Carefully lay specimens between two sheets of newspaper. Don't crowd or overlap the flowers or they will stick together. Make identifying labels for the flowers and put them between the papers close to the edge so that labels can be read without opening the pages. Stack the newspapers and weight them down with heavy books or bricks. Don't look for at least four weeks.

3 • To quick-dry your flowers, put them inside a folded sheet of waxed paper placed between sheets of newspaper and press with an electric dry iron set for synthetic material. Press for about 10 minutes; move the iron constantly so you won't burn the papers. Then place the ironed flowers between folded newspapers and weight them down overnight.

4 • Pressed and dried plants make pictures, bookmarks, placemats, and cards, or you can make a plant collection called an herbarium. Just glue the pressed plants to sheets of paper, identify the plants by their scientific and common names, and bind them together in a book. Loose-leaf or spiral notebooks make good herbarium books.

5 • To make a pressed flower picture, choose a picture frame and cut a sheet of paper to fit it. Lightly sketch the outline of the frame opening on the paper so

you won't glue flowers into the margin. Then arrange your flowers, leaves, and stems into a design *within* the margins. Use white, water-soluble glue. With a toothpick apply a small amount of glue to the back of each dried piece.

6 • When you have finished, set the picture aside and let the glue dry thoroughly before you put it in the picture frame. All dried pictures need a protective cover. Another way to protect your picture is to stretch clear plastic wrap over the flowers and tape it down on the back; if you use plastic wrap, choose heavyweight cardboard for the picture background or mount the picture on cardboard so the backing won't warp or bend when you stretch the plastic.

DRIED BOUQUETS

Air-dried Method

MATERIALS

flowers and plants
strong rubber bands

plastic or paper bags
mothballs

heavy-duty string   *container for flower arrangement*
coat hangers   *sand or styrofoam*

1 • Pick the flowers when the buds begin to open. Some flowers and plants that can be air-dried are listed below. Remove large leaves and gather a few stalks into a bunch. Secure the stalks with a rubber band a few inches from the bottom, attach a string, and hang them upside down from a coat hanger.

2 • Put your flowers in a warm, dry place (an attic or closet) for at least four weeks. If your plants have insects on them, put a few mothballs in a plastic or paper bag; put the bunch into the bag upside down, tie the open end, and then hang to dry.

3 • When the flowers are thoroughly dry, arrange them in a container partially filled with sand or a piece of styrofoam. Use large flowers first and fill in the spaces with small blossoms, leaves, and ferns. Punch holes in the foam before you insert the stems so they will not break.

PLANTS AND FLOWERS THAT WILL AIR-DRY:*

baby's breath	dock	sea thrift
bayberry	early goldenrod	sedges and grasses
Bells of Ireland	eucalyptus (branches	staghorn sumac
bittersweet	and pods)	statice
black alder	hazelnut	strawflowers
bottle brush	heather	tansy
cattail	hydrangea	thistle
celosia or cockscomb	marsh rushes	wheat
chinese lantern	milkweed pods	yarrow, common
corn	salvias	yucca

* Also look for other dried flowers, pods, and leaves standing on stalks or stems in pastures and fields and along roadsides, ponds, and fences in the fall.

Desiccant Method

MATERIALS

flowers

scissors

thin wire, No. 18 or 20 from hardware
store, cut in 8-inch lengths

toothpicks

white, water-soluble glue

large mixing bowl

box of white cornmeal

box of powdered borax (silica gel or
perlite will work, too) from grocery
store

nonmetallic containers with lids, such
as plastic or cardboard boxes

cotton balls

masking or florist tape

container for flower arrangement

sand or styrofoam

1 • Choose flowers with large, soft petals (see list below) and cut off the stems. Push one end of an 8-inch length of wire through the center of the flower. Bend a hook in the wire end above the flower and pull it back into the top of the flower's center. The wire will be your new stem. Flatten the wire so the flower will lie flat, petal-side up.

2 • To safeguard fragile petals, use a toothpick to put a few drops of glue at the base of the flower; let the glue dry before proceeding to step 3.

3 • Mix cornmeal and borax (5 parts cornmeal to 1 part borax) in a bowl. Spread a layer of the mixture in a box and lay the flowers face up. Carefully sprinkle the mixture over the flowers until they are buried. Don't crush the petals with a blob of mix. If a flower is cup-shaped, make a small mound of mixture and place the flower cup-side down over it, or fill the cup with cotton and then cover with the mixture.

4 • Put the box in a warm, dark, dry place for about three weeks. Dried flower petals feel crisp.

5 • Gently brush off the mixture when the plants are dry. Place a second length

of wire next to the first and bind the two together with masking tape or green florist tape. This makes a strong stem you can curve and shape. If petals fall off, just re-glue them.

6 • Put sand or foam in the bottom of a container and arrange your flowers and leaves. You also can give leaves a wire stem secured with tape. Dried bouquets use about twice as many flowers as fresh arrangements.

7 • If you keep the drying mixture in a sealed container, you can re-use it. If the borax becomes lumpy, dry it on a tray in an oven set for 150° F.

FLOWERS THAT WILL DRY IN DESICCANTS:

black-eyed Susan	*dahlia*	*feverfew*
carnation	*delphinium*	*hollyhock*
clematis	*dogwood*	*larkspur*

marigold   Queen Anne's lace   zinnia
peony   rose

SCENTED POTPOURRI

MATERIALS

flower petals—rose, lavender, lemon verbena, rose geranium, delphinium, phlox, or pansy
cake rack
airtight containers, such as a glass jar with a screw-top lid
measuring spoons

powdered spices—cinnamon, cloves, nutmeg, mace, allspice, etc.
dried grated lemon or orange peel
salt
perfume
decorative bottles, jars, or bowls with lids

1 • Collect petals of fully opened flowers before they fade. Scatter the petals on a cake rack and allow them to dry in a warm, shaded place. Let air circulate freely above and below the rack. Petals are ready to spice when they feel dry to the touch but not brittle. This may take as long as ten days.

2 • Put your potpourri in an airtight container such as a jar with a tight-fitting lid. Sprinkle about a half-inch layer of dried petals in the bottom and cover the petals with a sprinkling of salt, ½ teaspoon of mixed spices (choose the spices you like), and dried grated lemon or orange peel. Add another layer of petals, salt, spices, and dried peel; repeat until you use all the flowers or until you fill the jar. Sprinkle several drops of perfume on the last layer and tightly seal the jar.

3 • Store in a cool, dark closet for about two weeks. Then open and stir. Reseal the jar and store the potpourri for six to eight more weeks, stirring once a week.

4 • Put the aged potpourri in fancy glass jars, bottles, or bowls with lids. When you take off the lid, a delicious perfume will fill the room. Be sure to replace the cover to preserve your potpourri.

14

Puppets

Pioneer children owned few store-bought toys, but they made dozens of toys from things they found. They cut willow whistles and made elderberry popguns, whittled box traps and windmills, and smoked make-believe acorn and corncob pipes filled with sweet fern and cornsilk. Girls made fairy ladies gowned in piney petticoats, pine needle bracelets, baskets, and dollhouse brooms.

When spring came, children picked the first buttercups and held them under their chins. If yellow was reflected, that person loved butter. Down in the cornfields fierce armies waged mock battles with cornstalk spears and swords and made hideaway houses deep in the rows of stalks. Most boys played with handmade bows and arrows and banded together in hunting parties to chase squirrels and rabbits. They hunted for fun and seldom hit the mark.

Father and Mother made many family toys. Father whittled tiny wagons, small chests, toy chairs, and wooden dolls the children called puppets. Some puppets had hickory-nut heads or heads made from small gourds, baked dough, or even dried apples. Apple-head puppets looked like shriveled old grannies.

Mother sewed rag dolls with yarn hair and seed eyes and fashioned dried cornhusks into gentlemen and ladies with leafy bonnets and shawls. Perhaps Grandfather had made Mother's first doll. He had cut the body from a piece of deerskin, sewed the edges, and stuffed it with pine needles and sweet grass. She called it her Indian baby. Now she made rag babies for her little girls.

RAG DOLL

MATERIALS

sheet of newspaper
pencil
scissors
ruler
cloth the size your doll will be
straight pins
needle

strong thread
stuffing—cotton, socks, rags, etc.
two small round buttons for eyes
yarn
extra cloth for clothes
two hook-and-eyes for shirt

1 • Fold the sheet of newspaper in half and draw one side of the doll's body to make a pattern. Begin with the head and draw the neck, arms, body, and

legs the size you want the doll to be. Use the pattern shown on page 102 as a guide. Practice drawing the doll several times to get the shape you like. Cut out the pattern and unfold it.

2 • Fold the cloth in half and pin the paper pattern to it. Cut around the pattern. Cut the cloth larger than the pattern (about one inch larger on all edges) so you can sew up the seams.

3 • With right sides of the cloth facing each other, sew the seams. Leave about 3 inches open along one side of the body. Clip under the arms and at the neck almost to the seam line; see diagram p. 102. Turn the doll right side out and stuff it with cotton, cloth scraps, torn socks, or stockings. Sew up the hole.

4 • Use the two buttons for eyes and add a yarn mouth and nose, if you like. Cut uneven lengths of yarn for hair and sew them in place. Plaid or print material makes unusual rag dolls.

5 • Cut and sew simple trousers, shirts, blouses, and dresses for your doll. Use the patterns shown on page 102 as a guide; of course you will have to make the pattern larger to fit your doll. To make a shirt, cut two shirt fronts and one shirt back. Allow ¼ inch for seams and hems. With right sides together, sew the two fronts and the shirt back together at shoulders and sides. Hem the sleeves, neckline, and shirttail. Sew on two small hooks and eyes to close the shirt front.

To make overalls, follow the pattern and cut two pieces. Open flat and place the two pieces together with the right sides facing as in the diagram on page 102. Sew from #1 to #2 on each side. Then turn the overalls so that the seams you have sewn are at the center front and center back. Now sew the front of the pants to the back from #3 to #2 to #3 as indicated in the diagram on page 102. Hem the edges. Sew the front and the back together at one shoulder; turn the pants right side out and put them on your doll before tacking the second strap in place.

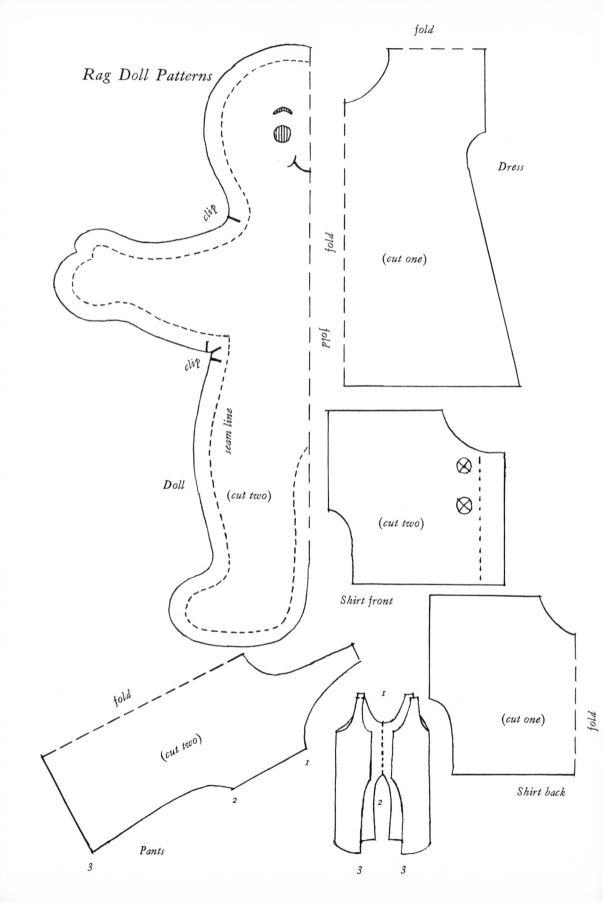

Rag Doll Patterns

fold

Dress

(*cut one*)

fold

fold

clip

clip

seam line

Doll

(*cut two*)

(*cut two*)

Shirt front

⊗

⊗

(*cut one*)

fold

Shirt back

fold

(*cut two*)

I

2

3

Pants

I

2

3   *3*

6 • To make a dress for your doll, cut out the dress pattern (all one piece) from a piece of cloth that has been folded twice; see diagram, page 102. Open, fold the dress in half lengthwise with the right sides together, and sew the underarm and side seams together.

Then cut the dress down the middle of the *back* from neck to hem. Hem sleeve, neck, and bottom edges. Then put the dress on the doll and sew the back opening closed. Tie a length of yarn or pretty ribbon in a bow around the waist and your rag doll has a long granny dress.

APPLE-HEAD DOLL

MATERIALS

a round, smooth apple

knife

lemon juice concentrate

bowl

string

wire, *10-* or *18-gauge from hardware store, cut into one 28-inch length and one 10-inch length*

scissors

cotton

roll of *1-inch-wide gauze or cloth cut*

into *1-inch-wide strips*

masking or adhesive tape

needle

thread

beads, seeds, or whole cloves for eyes

flat toothpicks for teeth

cornsilk, real hair, cotton, or yarn for hair

white, water-soluble glue

cloth for dress or shirt and pants

1 • Select a round, firm apple, not too ripe. Any apple will work, but Jonathan, Winesap, Red Delicious, and Rome are best. A Golden Delicious apple with its yellow skin gives the doll light-colored skin when it dries.

2 • Peel the apple and remove any bruised spots. Leave the stem and some apple peel around the top. Carve a nose, eye sockets, mouth, and ears. Exag-

gerate the features to allow for shrinkage, but do not cut too deep or the apple will rot near the core. The apple usually shrinks to one third or one half its original size.

3 • To give your doll a dark complexion, do not soak it in lemon juice. For a light complexion, use the lemon juice, which slows down the aging and gives the doll a lighter color. Pour the lemon juice concentrate into a bowl and submerge the apple. Do not handle the apple; use the stem. Soak the apple for about 45 minutes. As the apple absorbs the juice, it will sink. If the apple turns brown after you take it out, soak it some more.

4 • Hang the apple by the stem with a string in a warm, dry place away from the sun. A long drying time (about one month) will make a better doll, but if you want to shorten the time, hang the doll near the furnace. The drying will take about fifteen days. If the stem falls off, hang the apple on a wire. As the apple shrinks, the doll "ages." Wrinkles come naturally, but you can emphasize lines, eyes, and mouth with gentle pressure. Do not manhandle the apple.

5 • A dried apple looks like a deflated leather ball. The skin is tough but pliable. To form the body, cut a piece of wire 28 inches long and make a huge hairpin about five times the height of the apple head. One inch from the top of the hairpin shape, twist the wire three or four times. This makes a loop you can insert into the apple head, but wait until *after* you make the body to attach the doll's head. Separate and bend the two wire ends in opposite directions. Cut a piece of wire 10 inches long and lay it parallel and beneath the first piece of wire. Twist the long wire three or four times around the short wire to form the left shoulder. Do the same to make a right shoulder. Bend the long wire ends down and twist them together below the neck and shoulders. This forms the chest and waist. The remaining wire makes two legs. Form small loops in the wire ends for feet and hands. Adjust the wire arms and legs to sit or stand. You can cut the wire arms and legs to the length that best suits the head size. (See illustrations on p. 105.)

Apple-Head Doll

*Bend 28-inch length wire
into a large hairpin.*

*Twist wire into a loop
1 inch from the top.*

Bend the two wire ends in opposite directions.

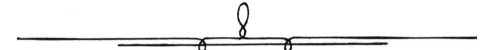

Lay 10-inch length wire beneath and parallel to first wire.

Twist long wire around short wire to make left and right shoulders.

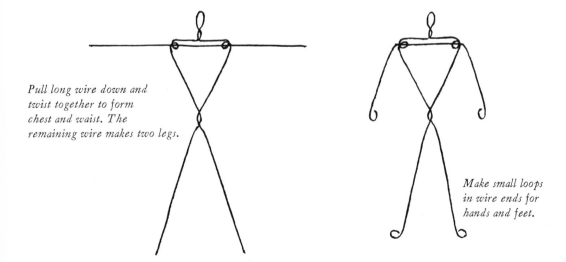

*Pull long wire down and
twist together to form
chest and waist. The
remaining wire makes two legs.*

*Make small loops
in wire ends for
hands and feet.*

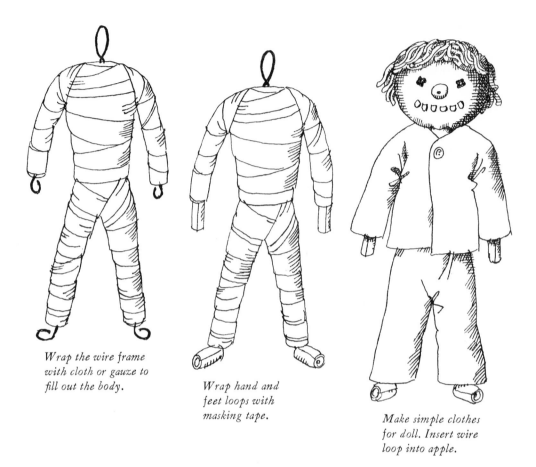

Wrap the wire frame with cloth or gauze to fill out the body.

Wrap hand and feet loops with masking tape.

Make simple clothes for doll. Insert wire loop into apple.

6 • To put meat on your wire bones, pad the frame with cotton or rags and use the gauze or cloth strips to hold the padding to the wire frame. Fasten the ends to the doll with tape or sew them in place. Wrap the feet and hands with masking tape. (See illustrations above.)

7 • Carefully push the looped wire neck into the back of the apple head so you will not mar the face.

8 • While drying, the eyes and mouth openings close, but you can gently open them to insert seeds, beads, or even whole cloves for eyes and flat toothpicks

for teeth. Break the toothpicks into small pieces and push them into the apple flesh. Add yarn, cotton, or real hair. Glue or push the ends under the apple peeling left on top.

Some apple-head dolls look like old men and others resemble women, so you can dress your doll with leftover cloth—pants and shirt for men, dresses and hats for women. If you make more than one doll, you can make scenes with dolls fishing, sewing, or playing games.

CORNHUSK DOLLS

MATERIALS

cornhusks and cornsilk

newspaper

scissors

large bowl with warm water

old bath towel

heavy-duty string, not too thick

pipe cleaner or lightweight wire for arms

white, water-soluble glue

needle

thread

cloth scraps for doll accessories

1 • Save the green husks and cornsilk when you have corn on the cob to eat, or collect shucks dried in the field on standing cornstalks. When you have fresh corn, separate the inner green leaves from the rest of the cornhusk, lay them on newspaper, and cover them with several sheets of newspaper. Allow the husks to dry until they turn light yellow. If you use dried in the field husks, also use only the smooth inner layers of leaves. Cut off the pointed tips and the stiff stem ends.

2 • Fill a large bowl with warm water. Soak the husks about 10 or 15 minutes to make them pliable. Keep the husks wet while you work. Always keep the smooth side of the husk turned to the outside.

3 • Lay a bath towel on your worktable to absorb excess water from the husks. Hold six or seven large husks together as if you were arranging them in layers all the way around an invisible stick. Tightly tie the bundle in the middle with strong string. Wind the string around the husks several times before you tie a knot, so the husks will not fall apart. Turn down the husks above the knot one by one as you would peel a banana. Pull the husks down until the ends are about even with the ends below the knot. Firmly wrap string around the husks and tie a knot about one inch from the top. The part above the knot will be the doll's head. (See illustrations on p. 109.)

4 • To make arms, roll a pipe cleaner or a piece of wire lengthwise in a large cornhusk. Turn the husk ends inside the roll to cover the wire tips as you roll. Tie the ends and the center with string. Do not make the arms too thick. Use only half a husk if necessary. (See illustrations on p. 109.)

5 • Separate the husks below the doll's head and push the arm piece between the layers under and against the head so the arms stick out at each side. Be sure to choose a smooth side of the head for the doll's face and keep it in front when you add the arms. (See illustrations on p. 109.)

6 • Roll a small strip of husk into a ball. Separate the husk layers just below the arms and fill the pocket with the rolled husk. Close the husks around the ball and tie them securely below the ball. Now you have a chest and waistline.

7 • Choose two wide cornhusk strips and drape one over each shoulder, crossing the strips in front and back. Tie string around the waist to fasten the ends. Cut a thin strip of husk about a quarter of an inch wide to cover the neck thread. Tie the husk off by making a knot or tying a bow in front. You can bend the arms to any position you choose. (See illustrations on p. 110.)

8 • To make the skirt, choose wide, soft husks and place them with the pointed ends at the waist and the wide stem ends over the head. Keep adding husks

Cornhusk Doll

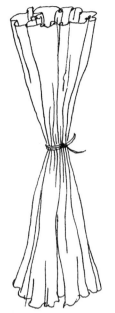

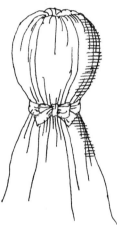

Cover thread with
thin strip of husk.
Tie knot or bow.

Lay 6 or 7
husks together.
Tie in the middle.

Turn down
husks above knot.

Tie a knot about
1 inch from top
for doll's head.

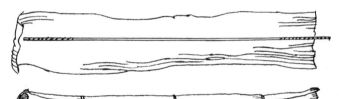

Roll wire in large husk
for arm piece.

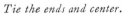

Tie the ends and center.

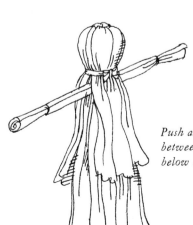

Push arm piece
between husk layers
below head.

Fill pocket below
arms with wad of
husk. Tie waist.

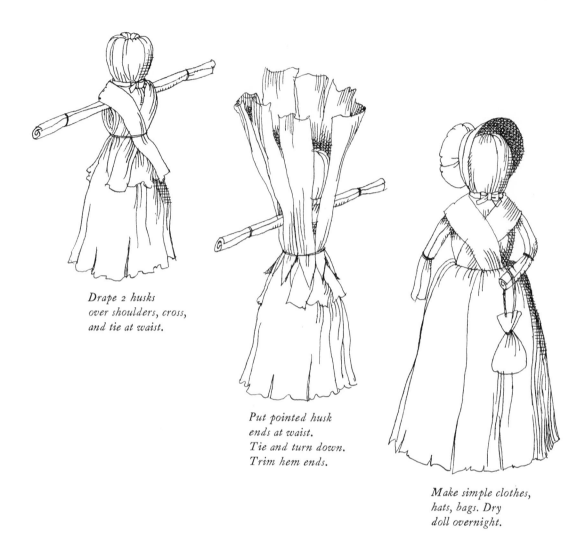

*Drape 2 husks
over shoulders, cross,
and tie at waist.*

*Put pointed husk
ends at waist.
Tie and turn down.
Trim hem ends.*

*Make simple clothes,
hats, bags. Dry
doll overnight.*

around the waist to make a full skirt. Then securely tie all the husks at the waist and turn down (toward the feet of the doll) the husk layers as you would peel a banana. Trim the ends that now form the skirt's hem to make them even so the doll can stand. (See illustrations above.)

9 • You can now braid, weave, or fold strips of husk to make shawls and bonnets, baskets or babies. Use your imagination. Glue or sew them in place.

Hide thread with thin strips of husk. Bits of cloth can become a bag or scarf, and small sticks can turn into brooms and rakes. To make hair, braid or drape wet cornsilk, shape and pin, then glue or sew it onto your doll.

10 • Allow the doll to dry overnight away from direct heat.

15

An Old-Fashioned Christmas

The very first colonists in America hardly celebrated Christmas. Shocked by the rowdy, boisterous holiday celebrations in old England, American Puritans even passed a law forbidding any observance of the holy day. In later years such restrictions faded, and the spirit of the season spread throughout the colonies.

German settlers cut evergreen trees and brought them inside to cover with candles, snowy popcorn chains, and big juicy red apples. Bethlehem Moravian colonists hung dozens of intricate white paper stars on their trees, and Dutch settlers decorated with hollow eggshells filled with tiny scenes, cookie wreaths, and gilded nuts. Christmas began in New Holland on December 6 when Dutch children filled their shoes with hay to feed the steeds of Saint Nicholas. He brought sweetmeats and fruit for good boys and girls and ashes and soot for bad ones. Southern colonists filled wassail bowls with hot Christmas grog, followed the hounds to the hunt, and gave small gifts to servants and tradesmen. French settlers in New Orleans religiously went to Christmas Eve Mass and saved their holiday merrymaking for New Year's Day when tables were loaded with juicy roasts, hot gravies, and plump pies. In Swedish settlements, settlers began Christmas on December 13 with the Festival of Lights to welcome St. Lucy, who brought sight to the blind and light to winter darkness. Birds of blond wool called chip-cuckoos hung in Swedish homes along with straw figures, animals, and stars, and bright colored crowing cocks rested on the mantels.

New World children eagerly waited for Christmas. When December winds brought the first snow, the children bundled up and left the house early to scour the hillsides. With promises that their Christmas celebration would last as long as the Yule log burned, they frantically hunted for the biggest log they could find.

Laughter and shouts echoed down the slopes as they poked under the snow kicking half-hidden stumps and rocks in their search. Soon a cry went up: "Over here! I found it." Everyone swarmed over the prize and helped truss and tie it up tight as a turkey ready for the spit. Then the big boys leaned into the tow ropes and dragged the Yule log down the hill followed by the others laden with holly, mistletoe, and ivy.

At home colonists baked fruitcakes and cooked mincemeat for holiday pies. Everyone helped to shape gingerbread dough into birds, animals, and toy soldiers for Christmas treats.

Christmas Tree Decorations

POPCORN AND BERRY CHAINS

MATERIALS

corn for popping
fresh, hard cranberries
large bowl
long, thin needle

heavy-duty thread
scissors
small buttons

1 • Pop the corn kernels and rinse the berries. Put them in a large bowl. Thread a needle with heavy-duty thread. Put a large knot in one end and string a button to hold the popcorn and berries on the thread.

2 • Run the needle through the berries lengthwise. Make white popcorn ropes or red cranberry chains or mix both on a chain. Join ropes and put a second button in the end.

SCANDINAVIAN STRAW ORNAMENTS

MATERIALS

clean straw (wheat is best, or try natural raffia or baled straw sold at feed stores)
newspaper
bowl of warm water
old bath towel

ruler
scissors
needle
strong red thread or thin string
white, water-soluble glue

Christmas Stars

1 • Gather straw in the field before harvest or purchase it in feed stores that sell baled straw for animals. If the straw is wet, lay it on several sheets of newspaper and cover it with another sheet to dry. Sort the dried straw into piles of the same size and color. Handle the straw carefully so you won't bend it. Dampen the straw in water before you begin, but don't soak it. Too much water weakens the straw.

2 • Lay a bath towel on your worktable to absorb moisture. Choose nine straws about 12 inches long and lay them on the towel side by side. Tie the straws tightly in the center with strong red thread or thin string, but don't tie them in a round bunch or you won't be able to fan the star's rays. Try to keep them side by side as shown in the illustration on page 117. Tie them again at about one-third of the distance from the center to each end.

3 • Now pick up nine straws, about 10 inches long, and tie in the center. Tie them about halfway between the center and one end; then between the center and the other end.

4 • Take nine more 10-inch straws and repeat step three. Now you have two bundles of 10-inch straws.

5 • Make an X with the two 10-inch straw bundles and lay them across the 12-inch bundle at the tie that is one-third of the way between the center and one end and tie all three bundles tightly together. Tie the 12-inch straw bundle again, halfway between the X and the top of the star.

6 • Separate the straw ends and fan them out. Make a slanted cut in the end of each straw. Pull a length of red thread through the straws on the back of the star and tie a loop to make a hanger for the ornament.

Scandinavian Straw Star

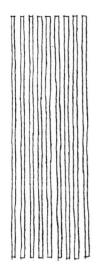 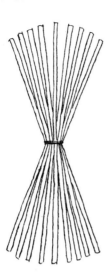  

Tie 9 10-inch straws
in center and
halfway between
center and each end.
(Make two.)

Lay 9 12-inch straws
side by side.

Tie in the center.

Tie again ⅓ of the
distance from the center
to one end. (Make one.)

Trim straws to the
angle shown.

  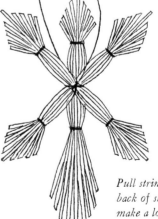

Make an X with the
2 10-inch bundles.

Tie again halfway
between the X and
the top of the 12-inch
bundle.

Scandinavian
Straw
Tinsel

Lay the straw X across
the 12-inch straw bundle
at the tie ⅓ of the
distance from the center
to one end. Tie.

Pull string through
back of star and
make a loop hanger.

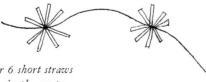 

Tie 4 or 6 short straws
together in the center.
Fan out from center.
Attach with knots to
length of cord.

Christmas Tinsel

1 • Choose four to six short pieces of straw and tie them together in the center. Bend the ends into a fan and make a slanted cut on each end.

2 • Cut a long piece of red thread for the rope, and tie the straw bundles to the thread 5 to 8 inches apart. (See illustration on p. 117.) You can drape this straw tinsel on the Christmas tree or use it with the evergreen and holly decorations in your home. The yellow sheen of clean straw gleams brightly under the Christmas lights. (Don't forget that the paper chains and snowflakes you learned to make in the papyrotamia chapter also make pretty holiday decorations.)

Straw Doll

1 • Cut about fifteen or twenty straws 16 to 20 inches long. Use enough straws to make a full skirt when you bend the straws in half.

2 • Hold the straws in one hand, and bend the bunch in half with the other hand. Wrap several turns of strong red thread or thin string around the straws about one inch below the bend. Tie a knot. This makes the head and neck. (See illustrations on p. 119.)

3 • Choose eight or ten more straws about 7 inches long for arms. Push this bundle of straws between the folded straws below the neck. Wrap with thread or string and tie below the arms to form the waist.

4 • Gently bend the arms down while carefully lifting the straws in the arms to shape shoulders. Wrap and tie the arms at both ends to form wrists.

5 • Fan the straws below the waist to make a full skirt for the doll. If you want to make a boy doll, divide the straw below the waist in half for two legs. Gently lift the straws to make full pants. Wrap and tie the legs to make ankles and feet.

Straw Boy and Girl

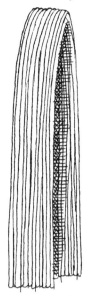

Bend straw bundle
in half.

Wrap straws about
1 inch below bend
for neck.

Push a straw bundle
between folded straws.
Wrap and tie below arms.

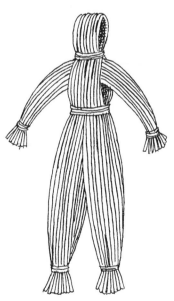

Wrap and tie wrists.

Fan straws below
waist for a skirt.

Or divide straws below
waist in half for
two legs. Wrap and
tie ankles.

6 • Glue down the loose ends of thread for a finished look. Slip a length of red thread through the straws on the back of the doll and tie a loop to make a hanger.

GINGERBREAD COOKIES FOR THE CHRISTMAS TREE

MATERIALS

mixing bowls

measuring cups and spoons

large spoon

electric mixer (optional)

floured board or kitchen counter

clear plastic wrap

rolling pin

cookie cutters or use cookie patterns shown in the book (To make cookie

patterns—scissors, pencil, sturdy cardboard)

sharp knife

spatula

cookie sheet

raisins

toothpicks

thread to hang cookies

colored icing (optional)

INGREDIENTS

1 stick of butter

½ cup white sugar or molasses

½ cup brown sugar

2 eggs

¼ teaspoon salt

½ teaspoon each cloves, nutmeg,

allspice (optional)

1 teaspoon ginger

1 teaspoon baking soda

2 teaspoons cinnamon

2½ cups all-purpose flour

1 • Cream until soft and light: 1 stick of butter, ½ cup white sugar or molasses, ½ cup brown sugar. Use an electric mixer or beat by hand.

2 • Add two eggs and beat thoroughly.

Gingerbread Cookie Patterns

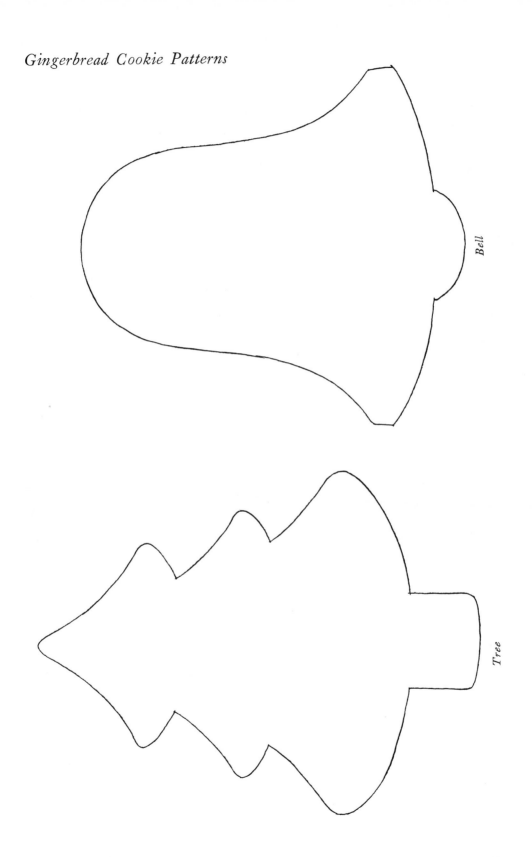

Bell

Tree

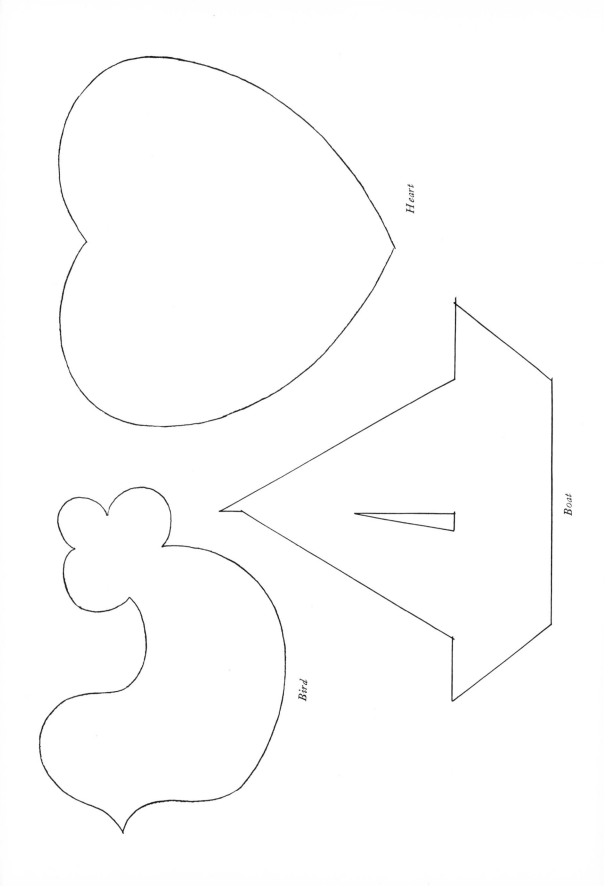

Heart

Boat

Bird

3 • Mix together: ¼ teaspoon salt; ½ teaspoon each cloves, nutmeg, allspice (optional); 1 teaspoon ginger, 1 teaspoon baking soda, 2 teaspoons cinnamon, 2½ cups all-purpose flour. Add this to the butter, sugar, and egg mixture.

4 • Beat until the mixer begins to clog or the dough lumps together. Turn the soft dough onto a floured surface. Add more flour, and knead the dough until it becomes smooth. Knead enough flour into the dough to make it stiff. Wrap the dough in plastic kitchen wrap and refrigerate it for at least 24 hours.

5 • Roll out a small amount of dough on a well-floured surface with a rolling pin. Roll the dough about ¼ inch thick. With cookie cutters or a knife, cut the dough into stars, birds, animals and trees, circles and hearts. Make giant gingerbread dolls or toy houses. To use the cookie patterns in the book, trace the patterns on sturdy cardboard, cut them out, and lay them on the rolled dough. Cut around the patterns with a sharp knife.

6 • Use a spatula to lift the figures onto a cookie sheet. Use raisins for eyes, mouths, and buttons. Break a toothpick into small pieces and stick one into each figure near the top to make a hole for string. Leave the toothpick in place and bake the cookies at 350°F. until they brown slightly, about ten minutes. Do not overbake or brown the edges.

7 • Remove the toothpicks and cool the baked cookies. Decorate them with colored icing, if you like. Then push thread through the holes and tie your cookies on the Christmas tree.

16

Sugaring Off

In March colonists waited impatiently for the west wind and maple-sugar time. With an eye on the winter sky, they busily scrubbed their barrels and spouts and stack of deep-dish wooden trenchers made from hollow logs. Then they loaded them on a sledge by the barn ready for a break in the weather when the first sap would run.

Sap rarely ran steadily. Sometimes it ran into April; sometimes it stopped and started again, but children could look forward to at least three or four days of frosty nights and mild days a-gypsying in the sugar camp. Soon they knew which trees ran the most sap and which ones gave the sweetest syrup. Like people, no two trees were the same.

The Indians taught the first European immigrants to tap trees, and later settlers followed their example. A diagonal slash was cut in the tree trunk, a hole bored, and a spout inserted to funnel the running sap into the trenchers propped at the base of the tree. All day sugar-bush workers and older children walked among the trees emptying sap from the trenchers into buckets that dangled from the ends of a yoke balanced across their shoulders. As the buckets filled, they poured the sap into a big kettle. The younger children fed the fire under it and watched the sap boil down into sugar.

The men and the older boys then poured the sugary syrup into partitioned tubs to harden. Each tub had a design in the bottom similar to a butter mold. When the sugar set, they removed the partitions, cut and wrapped the sugar cakes, and packed them in tubs for safekeeping. Colonists stored the second run of sap in large barrels as soft sugar. During the rest of the year, they drew off the dark sugar molasses for cooking and served it hot on griddle cakes.

At season's end, all the neighbors, young and old, came to the sugar grove for a sugaring-off party. While the hot syrup bubbled in the kettle, everyone played games, sang, and danced under the starry sky. When they tired, they poured the syrup on a patch of clean snow and greedily ate the chewy maple candy as soon as it cooled.

MAPLE SYRUP CANDY

MATERIALS

large pot or pan
long-handled wooden spoon
candy thermometer or cup filled with

ice water
large dishpan to be filled with snow or
    finely crushed ice

INGREDIENTS

1½ cups maple syrup

1 • Pour 1½ cups of maple syrup into a large pan with a heavy bottom so the syrup won't burn. Boil the syrup without stirring until it reaches the hard crack stage or 300° to 310°F.

2 • Measure the temperature with a candy thermometer. Place it near the center of the pan. Be sure the bulb does not touch the bottom of the pan or the reading will be incorrect. If you don't have a thermometer, drop a small quantity of syrup into a cup of ice water. If the syrup separates into hard, brittle threads, it has reached the hard crack stage.

3 • Fill a large pan with clean packed snow or finely crushed ice and slowly pour or spoon the hot syrup over it. The candy quickly cools into strips called "leather aprons," which you can pick up and eat. Try making a hard-packed snowball and dipping it into the syrup.

4 • Maple candy is very sweet so try sour pickles to cut the sweetness and you can eat much more. Donuts and hot cider make a real party. Boil more syrup as the candy disappears.

Epilogue

Every basket, candle, quilt, and doll this book teaches you to make is part of our American heritage. Each tells us something about the people who lived in a new world, far from old friends and old ways, and about the thousands of ordinary people—merchants, farmers, housewives, children—who settled the westward-moving frontier. These crafts and skills of every-day living are their remembrance to us, a sample of the way life was.

Selected Bibliography

HISTORY

Bernheim, Marc and Evelyne. *Growing Up in Old New England*. New York: Crowell-Collier Press, 1971.

Drake, Daniel. *Pioneer Life in Kentucky, 1785–1800*. New York: Henry Schuman, 1948.

Earle, Alice Morse. *Child Life in Colonial Days*. New York: Macmillan Company, 1899.
———. *Home Life in Colonial Days*. New York: Macmillan Company, 1898.

Gould, Mary Earle. *The Early American House: Household Life in America, 1620–1850*. Rutland, Vermont: Charles E. Tuttle Co., revised edition, 1965.

McGinnis, Ralph J., ed. *The Good Old Days: An Invitation to Memory*. New York: Harper & Brothers, 1960.

Needham, Walter, told by, recorded by Barrows Mussey. *A Book of Country Things*. Brattleboro, Vermont: The Stephen Greene Press, 1965.

131

Wigginton, Eliot, ed. *The Foxfire Book*. New York: Doubleday & Company, 1972.

CRAFTS

Carrick, Alice Van Leer. *Shades of Our Ancestors: American Profiles and Profilists*. Boston: Little, Brown and Company, 1928.

Creekmore, Betsy B. *Traditional American Crafts*. New York: Hearthside Press, 1968.

Foster, Laura Louise. *Keeping the Plants You Pick*. New York: Thomas Y. Crowell Co., 1970.

Simons, Amelia. *American Cookery*. Grand Rapids, Michigan: Wm. B. Eerdmans Publishing Co., 1965. (Reprint of the first American-written cookbook to be published in the United States by Hudson & Goodwin, Hartford, Connecticut, 1796.)

Webster, Marie D. *Quilts: Their Story and How to Make Them*. Doubleday, Page & Co., 1915.

Yates, Raymond F. and Marguerite W. *Early American Crafts and Hobbies*. Wilfred Funk, Inc., 1954.

CHERYL G. HOOPLE grew up in Lawrence, Kansas. She received a degreee in journalism from the University of Kansas and her M.A. in American Studies from the University of Hawaii. For several summers she organized and directed a camp craft workshop, experience she found invaluable in writing this book.

Ms. Hoople was formerly a professional field adviser and administrator for the Girl Scouts and a general reporter and feature writer for the Pensacola *News-Journal*. She is currently at work on a book about early America as seen through the eyes of female pioneers.

Cheryl Hoople lives with her husband and two young daughters.

RICHARD CUFFARI is a painter and the award-winning illustrator of numerous children's books. He was born in Brooklyn, New York, and studied at Pratt Institute. His work has been honored by the American Institute of Graphic Arts, the Society of Illustrators, and the Children's Book Showcase.

Mr. Cuffari lives in Brooklyn with his four children.